Special Friends
at Home

Sara J. Yoder

Christian Light Publications, Inc.
Harrisonburg, Virginia 22802

SPECIAL FRIENDS AT HOME

Christian Light Publications, Harrisonburg, Virginia 22802
© 2007 by Christian Light Publications, Inc.
Printed in the United States of America

Fifth printing, 2017

Cover art: Michelle Beidler
Cover design: David W. Miller

ISBN 978-0-87813-643-8

Publisher's Note

Those of you who have enjoyed Sara Yoder's books in the Benjie series will want to read *Special Friends at Home*. While this book is not part of that series, it includes some of the same characters.

The Amish teacher who wrote this story based it on actual incidents from her personal experiences. She relates them to bless the hearts of children.

Children are shown developing meaningful friendships by extending impartial friendliness to all they meet. Parents will appreciate the way the author portrays loving, respectful, family relationships.

Although the setting of this story is Amish, the lessons it instills apply to Christian families everywhere.

Books in the Benjie Series

by Sara J. Yoder

Benjie
Benjie Goes to School
Benjie, the In-Between Boy

Meet the Special Friends in This Book

Benjie Mast is an eight-year-old Amish boy who lives on a farm. Benjie loves the outdoors, and lots of activity and excitement. He likes to make new friends.

Ray Mast is Benjie's ten-year-old brother. He and Benjie are best friends. Ray loves to read and use big words.

Ellen Mast is Benjie and Ray's six-year-old sister. She loves to pretend being grown-up and taking care of her twin rag dolls.

Toby is two years old. He is the little brother the whole family enjoys.

Ruth is the baby, named after Aunt Ruth. Everyone loves baby Ruth.

Dad (David Mast). Dad keeps busy on the farm, but he is never too busy for his growing family. He wants their children to become God-fearing men and women.

Mom (Anna Mast). Mom is kept busy taking care of the family—sewing clothes, making meals, and tending the garden. Mom loves to keep everyone clean, neat, and happy. She supports Dad in teaching and training the children.

Uncle Marks (Mark and Ruth Miller). They live on the next farm and Aunt Ruth is Mom's sister. They have three children. Going to Uncle Marks is almost as special as going on a trip!

Nathan Miller is Ray's age and they are best friends, but they always want Benjie with them and include him in whatever they do.

Alta Miller is Ellen's age and they enjoy working and playing together. They never get tired of playing with their dolls.

Neil is Nathan and Alta's little brother. Neil had a twin sister that died at birth. Neil's family is very glad to have him.

Aunt Mandy is Anna Mast's great-aunt. Even though she is old and forgetful, Aunt Mandy still loves children and she still likes pancakes! Everyone loves Aunt Mandy. She lives with Uncle Alberts.

Danny, who has Down syndrome, is a very special boy. He loves to pretend he is an auctioneer selling cows, or a minister preaching a sermon. Danny never meets a stranger, because everyone is his friend. He lives with Uncle Alberts.

Al Camp is a tramp who loves pie, homemade bread, and coffee.

Elizabeth is deaf. Since she cannot hear, those who want to talk with her learn sign language.

Dedication

God bless all the dear children,
for whom this story was written.
Sara J. Yoder

Contents

Chapter 1

The Surprise

"Ray, come quick!" Benjie shouted as he burst into the house. "What do you think Dad brought home?" Benjie was shouting his news even though he could not see Ray. Benjie knew if Ray had his work done, he would be somewhere reading a book.

Just then Mom came out of the bedroom with Baby Ruth. Neither Mom nor the baby looked happy.

"Benjie," Mom reproved, "you woke Ruth. You need to learn to talk, not shout, when you come into the house." Mom shook her head and looked sadly at Benjie. "Sit on this chair for five minutes." She knew sitting on a chair was a grievous punishment for Benjie.

Benjie's face has a 'stricken' look, Ray thought as

he came into the room. Ray loved using new words. *Stricken* was one he had come across recently. It meant "hurt," for one thing. Ray could see Benjie felt hurt and distressed.

Benjie knew he must not talk back. This was not the first time he had disturbed Ruth's nap. He sat on the chair and looked at the clock. He loved his baby sister, but he kept forgetting about her naps.

"What did you want to tell me?" Ray asked in a kind, big-brotherly way.

Benjie looked at Mom.

"Yes, Benjie, you may talk." Mom knew what he was wondering. She sat down and started rocking Ruth back to sleep.

"Oh, Mom, when I am happy I feel like I have to shout! Dad brought home a surprise! But I am sorry I woke Ruth."

"A surprise?!" Ray exclaimed. "Where is Dad?"

"But Ray . . ." Then Benjie stopped and looked pleadingly at Mom. "Please, Mom, say that we can keep the surprise. Please! Dad said it depends on what you say."

"You mean you don't know what the surprise is either?" Ray interrupted excitedly.

"Not yet." Benjie looked at Mom. His eyes begged her to say yes. "Please, Mom."

Mom was looking curious, but rather doubtful. "If it is a goat, I don't know where we would keep one. And with Uncle Mark's goats breaking

2

out and coming over, we would have a regular mix-up with goats." Mom was shaking her head as she spoke. Already she was, as Ray would say, "fearing the worst."

"And the garden," Mom went on, "I do not want goats in the garden." Mom was even now picturing a herd of goats frisking about in her precious garden, eating everything in sight.

"Oh, it isn't a goat." Benjie stared hard at the clock. "Mom, is it five minutes?"

Mom glanced at the clock and nodded. "Yes, it is, Benjie, and you may go."

"I will try to remember not to forget," Benjie said as he hurried out with Ray. For Ray had waited for him, not wanting to go out without Benjie. Ray dearly loved his younger brother. Even though they were natured differently, they were very good friends. Ray loved to study and read. Benjie loved to be outdoors. He did not like to read. Not if he could go exploring in the woods, or be outside where things happened in real life instead of on a written page! How he hated sitting on a chair and doing nothing! A whole day did not seem as long as those five minutes, sitting there staring at the clock and thinking about why he had to be punished.

Even as he hurried outside, he whispered a little prayer that God would help him remember. He loved Mom and did not want to disappoint her.

3

Shep, their faithful old dog, bounded to meet the boys. Then he saw Mom coming with Ruth. At once Shep turned his attention to Mom, wagging his tail joyfully. Shep loved them all, but, as Ray once said, it seemed Shep knew Mom was special, for he was always extra happy when he saw her.

Whenever Dad came home, Shep barked and welcomed him joyfully. Shep was never out of humor when he was awakened from a nap. Now he went from one person to the other, wagging his plume of a tail and smiling his big dog smile.

Ellen and Toby left the sandbox where they had been playing and came to join the rest of the family. Ellen was just younger than Benjie. She loved to pretend that Toby (who was not quite three) was her little boy. She held his hand and walked slowly so he could keep up.

By now Dad had finished unharnessing Chap, their new horse. As soon as Dad turned him out, Chap rolled himself in the pasture. Since it had rained a little shower that morning, Chap was soon covered with dirt. But he did not mind. He shook himself heartily several times and galloped out to join the other horses.

"How do you like Chap by now?" Mom asked as Dad came near. Ray and Benjie looked at each other. They were fairly bursting with curiosity, and now their parents had to discuss Chap! The boys loved horses, but the horse was not the surprise.

4

"He did well," Dad said, answering Mom's question. He had gotten Chap several weeks before at a sale. "The owner didn't want him because he didn't ride well, remember? But he did just fine with the wagon."

"Good. You'll use him more for pulling the wagon and the buggy anyway," Mom said. "If he is safe and stands quietly, that is the main thing."

"But, Mom, we wouldn't want to drive just any old plug, would we?" Ray asked. Ray liked a horse that had speed.

"Couldn't we talk about horses later and get on with the surprise?" Benjie asked impatiently. He knew he must not interrupt grown-ups, but Ray was not a grown-up.

"Oh, yes, the surprise," Dad said, with a twinkle in his eye. He picked up a box from under the wagon seat. He brought it over to Mom and then hesitated.

"If we don't keep the surprise, maybe it is best we don't see it," he said.

Dad looked at Mom, and Mom looked at Dad.

"If it's a good surprise, we'll surely keep it," Mom said, relieved that it did not seem to be a goat. "I can't imagine what it is." She was curious too.

The box quivered a little in Dad's hands, and low whimpers came out of it.

"Oh, what is it?" Ray and Benjie asked together. Dad set the box on the ground. Ellen and Toby crowded close to it. Toby started to reach for the flap, but just then a little puppy bounced out!

"He must have gone to sleep on the way over," Dad said, "but he certainly is awake now."

No one knew what to say for a moment. He was the cutest puppy Benjie had ever seen. Then Toby clapped his little hands and laughed. Ellen wanted to hold the puppy.

"What would be a good name for him?" Ray asked. Surely if they named him right away, that would mean they could keep him!

The puppy wagged all over with friendliness. His tail wagged as fast as a puppy dog's tail can wag. He tried to jump up on Benjie and then on Ray. He scampered around Toby. Then he saw Shep and bounded over to him. Maybe he thought Shep was his mother. He was so happy to see Shep.

Shep only stood and stared at the puppy. He did not smile his friendly dog smile. He did not wag his tail. In fact, his long plumy tail drooped low. When the puppy started playing with him, Shep uttered a low little growl and showed his teeth. He knew he must not hurt the puppy. But it was plain that Shep was not pleased with a puppy there.

"What is wrong with you, Shep?" Mom scolded.

"Maybe he is jealous." Dad shook his head.

"All these years he has been the only dog on the farm."

Poor Shep felt he was in disgrace. With his head and tail hanging low, he crept off to his hole under the hedge.

All these years he had been a faithful dog. When it was time to bring in the cows, Shep was there to help Benjie round them up.

When the calves escaped from their pen, Shep let his people family know by his sharp barks. Shep never hurt the kittens or chased the cats. Nor would he chase a mother hen or baby chicks. Some dogs would chase and kill chickens — but not Shep.

If anyone came, day or night, Shep would let the family know by his bark. And Shep seemed to know when there was an opposum in the henhouse. He patrolled the farm and had killed more than one rat.

When Toby pulled at his tail or ears, Shep would bear it patiently. He would never hurt the children or snap at them.

There was no way of knowing what went on in Shep's dog mind, but it was plain that he was very unhappy with Dad's surprise.

Ray and Benjie wanted desperately to keep the puppy. But now they felt so sorry for Shep they didn't know what to think.

"I'm afraid Shep feels we are going to supplant him with this new pup," Ray said. He did feel bad for Shep, but he couldn't help enjoying the importance of using another new word.

"Whatever does *supplant* mean?" Benjie asked, annoyed. He often felt impatient with his brother's new words. He knew whenever he could not find Ray, he would be somewhere reading a book and coming across even more new words.

"You know people don't plant dogs," Benjie added, sounding disgusted.

"Of course not. It means "to replace." When Dad needs a new wagon he supplants the old one with a new one." Ray enjoyed explaining new words to Benjie.

"I know what *replace* means," Benjie said.

"Well, likely Shep feels we are replacing him with the puppy," Ray said.

They both walked over and talked to Shep and stroked his head.

"Shep," Benjie declared, "we would never replace you for a hundred puppies. You are the best dog around."

Shep wagged his tail a feeble little wag or two. He politely licked at Benjie's hand. Then he put his head down between his paws and mourned. It was plain that Shep was deeply hurt.

"He will likely get over it in a few days," Dad said, although he felt sorry for Shep too. "He will get used to the puppy and forget his hurt feelings."

8

Then Dad remembered. "That is, if we keep the puppy." He looked inquiringly at Mom.

Mom looked at Dad and then at the children. She thought of the garden and the flowers. She thought of how puppies dig holes and pull at wash on the line. She thought of shoes and toys that get chewed up or carried away if they are left outside. She thought of the hens and the baby chicks. There was no way of knowing what all a puppy would get into. Mom looked again at the puppy, who seemed to be fairly begging to be loved by this family. Mom really liked puppies, too, but being a busy mother with children gave her other things to consider as well.

On the other hand, a puppy was just like God made it. A puppy was so happy, it made you feel happy. A puppy could help teach children responsibility. A puppy could entertain children for hours. Having a puppy could be so special, because there is nothing quite like a wriggling, lovable, little puppy.

Mom looked at Ray and Benjie. "He will take watching and training," she said, thoughtfully.

"I'll do my best!" Ray's voice was eager.

"Oh, yes, I'll help!" *That would be fun,* Benjie thought.

"Where did you get him?" Mom asked, looking at Dad.

"I was almost in town when a car stopped and a man climbed out holding him. The man said he was going to put him off beside the road. But when he passed me, he decided to stop and ask if I'd take him."

"What?" Mom looked distressed. "Just dump a helpless puppy off beside the road?"

"That is right." Dad did not look happy either. "That is what some people do. They dump off dogs and cats they don't want or don't have room for. Then the animals have to hunt for food or starve."

"I can't see how anyone could treat baby animals like that," Mom said. She could never stand to see an animal hurt or hungry.

"It would be far more merciful to kill them right away than to have them running around crazy with hunger or starving to death," Dad agreed. "No farmer wants wild dogs on his farm. But that is what happens if puppies or dogs are abandoned and have to fend for themselves."

"Banded," Benjie mumbled. He peered at the wiggling puppy. "This one isn't."

"Isn't what?" Ray asked.

"He isn't banded. There's no band on him."

"Listen, Benjie," Dad explained. "I said 'abandoned.' It means 'deserted, or forsaken.' A puppy left to himself is quite forsaken. He is all alone. Unfortunately, puppies are not the only living creatures that get abandoned. Sometimes fathers abandon their children or a mother abandons her baby. That is terrible. God planned

10

for children to grow up securely in their homes, receiving love and acceptance as well as training and teaching. But sometimes parents do not follow God's ways, and do not care about their children. Or, sometimes a mother, who does not want to abandon her baby, realizes she is unable to care for him, and so she will leave him somewhere she thinks he will be cared for."

"Abandoning babies is more frequent in places where people are very poor," Mom added.

Benjie looked at Ruth, who had fallen asleep in Dad's arms. "How could anyone ever give their baby away?"

"Sometimes I think it must take a special kind of love for a mother who knows she is unable to care for her child, to put that baby in a home where it *will* be cared for. But that," Dad explained, "is very different from abandoned children, whose parents just deserted, or left, them."

Benjie was thinking. How would it be if no one cared for *him*? He could not imagine how anyone could ever abandon a puppy, much less a baby. The very thought made him feel like he had to cry. He rubbed his hand over his eyes, pretending they were itchy.

"We will keep the abandoned puppy," Mom was saying. "There is no danger that he won't get enough love here."

Chapter 2

Al Camp

"Life will certainly be different with a puppy on the farm," Ray remarked as Benjie and he walked in from the barn after chores the next morning. The puppy scampered along at their heels. "But what are we going to name him? We don't want just any name."

"No. Not just any old name. We want a good one," Benjie agreed. "He is brown, but Brownie is such a common name."

"That is true. Maybe Cousin Nathan would know a good name."

Shep had already followed Dad to the house. When the boys approached with the puppy, Shep moved away with a disapproving, hurt air. It was plain that he did not want to have anything to do with the puppy. In fact, he acted insulted.

But the puppy did not know that. He bounded over to Shep and tugged at his tail and pretended to bite it. He pawed at Shep and barked little puppy barks. Shep knew he must not growl at this little dog. But he looked down at him and made an unfriendly grimace with his mouth.

"Good boy, Shep. Good old Shep," Ray cheered. "You know enough not to hurt the puppy. Maybe in a few days you will be used to him."

Shep looked up at Ray sadly.

Benjie patted Shep's head. "You will always be our very best dog, Shep. We'll never supplant you." He petted him some more and Shep whined a low, pleased whine. Then he looked at the puppy who was still pulling and tugging at him. Shep looked back up at Benjie. His look said plainly, "Why must I put up with this scamp?"

When Benjie stopped petting him, Shep rose with a much injured air, and moved to his hole under the hedge. He was not a happy dog. He put his head down on his paws and "brooded," as Ray put it.

"And that means," Ray explained to Benjie, "that he is fretting or worrying about something. And in this case, it's the puppy."

Benjie looked at Shep sorrowfully. Shep was such a good dog, and now in his old age, Shep felt they liked the puppy better than they liked him.

"I hope he doesn't get sick and die," Benjie said at breakfast.

"I think he'll be okay," Dad said. "Sometimes people act that way too." Dad took a piece of bread and spread butter on it.

Benjie looked up from his egg and bacon. Benjie always enjoyed breakfast. Bacon and eggs went together, just like pancakes and syrup. And Dad had cured the bacon. They all thought it was extra good. Sometimes Mom served sausage with the eggs instead of bacon. Benjie could never decide which he liked better. Then on Saturday mornings, there would be pancakes. There were so many good things Mom could make for breakfast. But this morning Benjie hardly noticed what he was eating. He was feeling sorry for Shep.

He thought about what Dad said. "You mean people act like dogs?" he asked.

"People fret and worry too." Dad was cutting up Toby's egg so he could eat it better. "And Shep acts hurt and jealous because he is not getting the attention he used to get. Remember how Toby acted when we first had Baby Ruth? He would do things for attention."

Dad looked at Benjie to see if he understood. Benjie looked very thoughtful. Dad went on. "It's not just little children that want attention. Grown people get jealous too, or their feelings get hurt. Everyone likes to be appreciated, but if we don't get that appreciation it is easy to feel left out, or hurt, or jealous."

Benjie nodded. Sometimes he felt that way.

Ray could do so many things he could not do. And there were times when Ray and Cousin Nathan spent time together and he felt left out. Not that they did it on purpose, Benjie just did not have a cousin his age.

"So that is how Shep must feel!" Benjie exclaimed. He decided to do all he could to make Shep know he was appreciated and loved.

"Remember when Shep was hurt?" Ray was saying. "The time a car hit him, and the vet came and gave him a shot?"

"The vet said your love and care for Shep was what pulled him through," Mom recalled, smiling at Ray and Benjie. "That is the secret for us all—loving and caring. Isn't it?"

"It is," Dad agreed. "Because we love God, God in turn gives us a love for others, even those who seem unlovable."

Benjie thought about that. Then he thought of Enos Yoder. He had to try really hard, and even then it was not easy, to really like Enos. Enos was his age and in his grade in school. Sometimes Enos was just as nice as could be. Then Benjie found it easy to like him. But when Enos played mean tricks on him, that was something else.

Then he thought of Tobias, the tramp who had visited them last summer. "Was our tramp an unlovable man?" Benjie asked. Then he hastily added, "But I like him. I wish he would come again."

15

"Yes, some people would feel Tobias was unlovable," Dad answered. "But no matter who comes our way, we want to remember God loves that person too."

No one in the family had any idea who was going to come to their door that very day!

It was Benjie's turn to help Ellen with the dishes. As soon as that task was done, Benjie planned to go out to Shep and make him feel appreciated. Much as he loved the bouncing puppy, he would not neglect Shep. No, indeed!

Dad and Ray were putting on their hats to go out. Mom was still feeding Baby Ruth her breakfast. Toby was already out in the sandbox digging holes.

Benjie heard a car stop and then start up again. Curiously he peeked out the window. He could not believe his eyes, for at first he thought it was their tramp, Tobias.

It was not Tobias, however, but it *was* another tramp. He carried a black satchel, not a brown one like Tobias did. This tramp was stocky, and he walked briskly as he came up to their door.

Ray and Benjie looked at each other. Ray was thinking how surprised Cousin Nathan would be to hear about another tramp. And who knew what might be in his black satchel! Maybe this man was a spy in disguise. Maybe he was an outlaw. A fugitive fleeing from justice. Fugitive meant the same as a runaway, but a fugitive sounded more exciting. Under his breath, Ray was muttering, "Likely a fugitive."

The tramp climbed the steps to the porch. The Masts were all quiet, fairly holding their breath. Dad went to the door and opened it.

Perhaps Dad was remembering what he had said just a moment ago, how one should love everybody. His voice was kind as he said, "Hello."

The man set his satchel on the porch and took off his cap.

Tobias, the other tramp, always had a rusty, worn-out look. This man looked younger, though still older than Dad. His coat looked old, but his shoes were sturdy. He spoke in a deep, slow voice.

"Hello," he responded. His eyes met Dad's. "I am looking for work."

"Well," Dad began. He pulled at his beard. When he did that, he was thinking hard. It was plain that he was not sure what to say. He glanced over at Mom, who was holding Ruth. Mom looked uncertain too. Who was the man? Could he be trusted?

Ray and Benjie waited anxiously. What would Dad decide?

"Well," Dad said again, stalling for time. "You want work for today?"

"No, I am looking for a steady job," the tramp

replied. "I would need meals and board out of my pay."

"I see." Dad looked at Mom again. Mom's look said, "Do whatever you think." But they were both thinking, *Can we trust him?*

Suddenly Dad's voice became sure and steady. "Very well. We will give it a try."

There were many jobs around the farm that Dad needed to do but did not get done—a fence to build, a ditch to dig, trees to prune. Yes, there was plenty of work.

"Have you had breakfast?" Dad asked.

"I had breakfast."

"And your name?" Dad hesitated. "What shall we call you?" *Maybe the stranger did not want to say what his name was. If he was a spy in disguise,* Ray was thinking, *he would not want to tell them his real name.*

"My name is Al Camp," the man said. "Just call me Al."

Ray took a deep breath and looked closely at the man. *Al could be short for many different names. Maybe there was a mystery about Al.* Ray could hardly wait to tell Nathan about him.

"We don't have an extra room, but we will fix a place for you to sleep," Dad said. He picked up his hat. "And now, if you are ready to work, we will go out and start on the fence."

As soon as they left, Ellen and Benjie got busy. Never had they washed dishes so fast. Benjie did not want to waste a minute in the house. Not with such an exciting tramp on the place!

Benjie quite forgot about Shep. And Shep, after inspecting the tramp in dog fashion, went back to his hole under the hedge. The puppy, meanwhile, wandered out to the barn and worried the kittens. Engine, the good-natured black cat, would just sit and watch the puppy, but the mother cat would spit and hiss until the puppy backed off.

When Benjie came out of the house, Al was already working on the fence. Dad and Ray were coming out of the barn.

"Now Benjie," Dad said in an undertone, even though he was quite a distance from Al, "do not bother Al with questions. It is all right if he talks to you, but he may not want to talk about himself. You or Ray may bring him a drink every so often. He will get thirsty working like this."

"Yes, Dad. How long do you think he will stay? May I ask him where he is going after he leaves here? Do you think he has met our other tramp?" Benjie stopped for breath. He was bursting with questions.

"I don't know how long he will stay. But like I said, do not ask him questions. And it's hard telling if he has ever met Tobias."

When Ray and Benjie took a drink out to Al, they both hoped with all their might that Al would ask *them* some questions, but he didn't.

He silently took the glass and drank the cold water. It was plain that Al was a man of few words, and Ray was convinced there was a mystery about him.

The boys could hardly wait until dinnertime. Surely Al would talk then!

Dad noted that Al did not work fast, but he worked steadily and kept at the job. After all, you could not expect a man of his age to work with the speed of a young man.

At the table, Al ate the way he worked. Not fast, but he kept at it. Before eating, they had bowed their heads for silent prayer. Then Dad passed the bread. Al took a thick slice of Mom's good, homemade wheat bread. He spread it generously with butter and strawberry preserves. They all noted the smile of enjoyment on his face. It was the smile and look of a man wholly content.

Then Al looked up. "Have you coffee?" he asked.

Mother looked a little startled. "Why, yes. I have instant coffee. I can make some."

In no time at all, Mom had water boiling and soon set a cup of coffee before Al. His smile of content grew more noticeable.

And all the while Dad was (as Ray said later) being sociable. He talked and tried to draw Al into the conversation, but Al was too busy eating. Dad passed the food around again, and Al took generous second helpings. He took a second slice of bread as well. Benjie watched, fascinated. Al ate more than he and Ray together!

For everyday meals they sometimes had a simple dessert of cookies and fruit. Mondays there was usually pie or something left from Sunday dinner. Today, Mom offered peaches and cookies. Al carefully took two cookies with his serving of peaches.

When that was eaten he looked up. "Have you pie?"

Then the children forgot their manners, and stared at Al. *A grown man, asking for pie!*

Mom looked flustered and a little shocked. "We don't have any pie."

"Then I will take another piece of bread."

So Dad passed the bread again. Al carefully spread butter and jam on another piece. Looking up, he asked, "Have you more coffee?"

Quickly Mom fixed another cup for him. They all waited patiently while Al finished eating his last piece of bread and drank his coffee.

This was very different, Benjie thought to himself. Usually, he or Toby was the last one to finish eating, and everyone had to wait on him. And besides, never had he seen a grown man that would ask for pie!

"He is not polite, is he?" Ellen said when they were washing the dishes.

"Well, tramps are in a class by themselves," Ray said wisely. For a long time he had waited for an opportunity to use that expression. Now it just fit the situation. "Tramps do and say things differently because they are tramps."

Mom returned from putting Ruth and Toby to bed for their naps. In the washhouse, Dad was fixing the screen door. Al was walking out to the pasture where he was making fence.

Leaving his work for a little, Dad came into the kitchen. Looking at Mom, he said, "Don't feel bad because you didn't have any pie." There was a little twinkle in Dad's eye.

Mom had to smile, even while she looked a little grim. "Do you think he will eat us out of house and home?"

"We'll see." Dad leaned against the counter. "If he stays he will have to be content with the everyday fare we have. But he can hardly do without his coffee."

Mom nodded. "I can easily make that for him."

"If his work is satisfactory and you don't mind the extra cooking," Dad said, "it will help me catch up, and give him a lift too."

"I don't mind. The poor man. I am glad if we can do something for him," Mom said. "It will be nice if he can help you. Should we fix up a room in the basement for him?"

"Since it is cemented we could do that. Or would he be more comfortable in the wood-house?"

"Why don't we let him choose, that is, if he wishes to stay?"

The children were listening breathlessly. There was no telling what adventures they might have with Al Camp there!

"Let's do that," Dad agreed. He turned to the children. "Remember, boys, be friendly and polite to Al. And don't use the word *tramp*. We don't want to look down on anyone, no matter who they are. God is no respecter of persons. The poorest tramp is just as important to God as the richest man or greatest king on the earth. Each soul is precious."

"Jesus loves him, doesn't He?" Ellen asked. She had been listening just as intently as Ray and Benjie.

"Indeed He does. And we don't want to feel we are better than anyone else."

"Maybe we can even be friends," Benjie said hopefully. He was always on the outlook for friends.

"Won't Nathan be surprised when we tell him about Al Camp!" Ray exclaimed. He and Benjie looked at each other and smiled. They could hardly wait to talk to Nathan!

Chapter 3

A Visit From Nathan

When Cousin Nathan found out a few days later that Ray and Benjie had a puppy, he wanted to go see it right away. There were so many things that needed checking out. What kind of puppy was it? Just where had they gotten it? Who was the man who was going to heartlessly drop it off beside the road? Nathan thought that would have been a lowdown thing to do. And Nathan's mother, who was Ray and Benjie's Aunt Ruth, said abandoning animals should be against the law. Aunt Ruth could not bear to see any animal hurt or hungry.

Nathan did not actually *ask* to visit Cousin Ray, but in roundabout ways he tried to arrange it. When his mother could not find her long-handled dipper, Nathan readily offered to go see if it was at Ray's house.

But right away his younger sister Alta spoke up. "We needed it in the sandbox," she said. "We wanted to pour sand into a can."

Aunt Ruth was not happy about that. "Do not take anything from the kitchen unless you ask me first," she reproved. "There is no telling what might have happened to that dipper, besides getting dirty and germy."

"Mother, you always think of germs." Alta could not understand how germs could be so terrible. "We can wash them off, can't we?"

"Yes, we can wash the dipper," Mother replied. "But depending on what germs you get, you can get very sick."

"Yes, Mother," said Alta, nodding. Then she ran out to get the dipper.

The next day Aunt Ruth wanted to sew a dress for Alta. She selected a few spools from her sewing basket and laid the thread against the material. "Well now, isn't that disappointing," she lamented. "I don't have any thread that matches."

Nathan had just come into the house for a drink. "Why, I know what!" he exclaimed. "I could take a sample over and see if Aunt Anna has some."

Aunt Ruth stopped what she was doing and looked at Nathan. All day yesterday Nathan had offered, for every little thing, to go over to Uncle David's house. Why hadn't she thought of it before? Nathan wanted to see the new puppy. She thought for a bit.

"Have you finished cleaning the feed room?" she asked.

"It's all done, Mother."

"Well, I would be glad to have that thread. Here is a sample of the fabric. If Aunt Anna has something that almost matches, she can send it."

Aunt Ruth looked at Alta, who was listening eagerly.

"Please, Mother," she whispered.

"Yes, Alta, you may go too." Aunt Ruth looked at the clock. "I see it is nearly dinnertime. We'll have dinner early, and then you may go, both of you."

Right after dinner, Nathan and Alta started out in high spirits. No matter how often they visited Uncle Davids, it was always special. And for once, no one saw them coming, for Uncle Davids were having a late dinner. Nathan knocked at the door. When his aunt opened it, she exclaimed, "Why, Nathan and Alta! What a surprise!"

Aunt Anna ushered them into the kitchen to join the rest of the family. Immediately they noticed a stranger sitting at the end of the table.

Who is he? Nathan wondered. *If I had known Uncle Davids had company today, I would have waited until later to visit.*

But Aunt Anna did not allow him time to

worry about that. She bustled around, pulling two extra chairs up to the table.

"Here," she was saying, "Alta can sit beside Ellen, and Nathan can squeeze in between Ray and Benjie. Surely you two have room for some custard pie." She brought two clean plates from the cupboard. "The hens are laying so well I decided to make some custard pies," she said.

Dad made some quick introductions. "Nathan, Alta, this is Al Camp," he said. "Al, these children are my wife's niece and nephew."

Al looked silently at the children. "I see," he said in his slow way. He took a sip of his coffee.

Mom had cut the delicious-looking pie into pieces. She helped Ellen and Alta take some. Then she handed the pie to Al. Al looked at the pie and smiled. Carefully he took a generous piece. Without him asking, Mom refilled his coffee cup. She knew he would soon have asked for more.

"Al is doing some work for us," Dad explained.

Nathan nodded. He was full of questions, though he knew it was not polite to ask them now. But sitting across from Al allowed Nathan to watch him without seeming rude. Al, he noticed, ate with the utmost concentration.

"Yes, that describes it," he later told Ray. "And that means," he explained to Benjie, "to focus all your attention on what you are doing."

When they had eaten a whole pie and part of a second one, Dad politely passed the pie around again. Al carefully helped himself to another large piece.

Everyone waited patiently until he finished eating his pie and drinking his coffee. Even when he was done, he kept holding the handle of the coffee cup, looking at it with deep regard.

After dinner, when Al returned to his work, Ray and Benjie took Nathan to the woodhouse where Al slept. On the way, they answered Nathan's questions about Al.

Mom and Ellen had made the woodhouse nice and comfortable. There was the cot, fixed neatly as always. Al's black satchel, closed as usual, sat in its normal place on top of the cot.

"If we could just look in that satchel, maybe it would explain some things," Nathan said.

"I know," Ray agreed. "But Al always keeps it closed."

"Maybe I could take just one peep," Benjie said. He had often wondered what all was in it. Tobias, the other tramp, had had a satchel too. What did tramps keep in them?

"Don't you even think of doing such a thing!" Ray scolded. "There is no telling what could happen."

"What could happen in a black satchel?" Benjie asked, feeling more curious than ever.

"Who knows? Maybe there is a hidden trap in

it," Nathan said. He loved mysteries.

"Yes," Ray agreed. "Or if he is a spy, he might be keeping a record of everything that happens. He would be certain to know if we snooped in his bag. Besides, it would be very mean of us to snoop in someone else's belongings. Not that I wouldn't like to look in it myself," he added.

They were so busy talking and surmising about Al Camp that Nathan forgot he wanted to see the new puppy.

The puppy had been taking a nap in the barn, but now he was ready to play. He found Ellen and Alta playing with rag dolls in the yard, and frisked around them for awhile. But when the boys came out of the woodhouse, he bounded over to greet them. The girls followed more slowly, to see if their brothers were doing any-thing exciting.

After tussling with the puppy briefly, Nathan asked, "What is his name?"

"We need help picking out a nice name," Ray answered. "Any ideas?"

"I think he has the markings of a good dog," Nathan observed. "Who knows? You might have a valuable dog someday. Now, a good name for him . . ." Nathan stopped to think. "What about Rascal?" he suggested.

Ray looked thoughtful. "Well, *rascal* means 'a dishonest person.' We want a name our puppy can live up to."

"What about Tippy?" Alta asked.

"Well," Benjie spoke up, "Ellen thought of that too, but Tippy sounds more like a house dog."

Ellen and Alta looked at each other. They both felt it would be more fun to play with the rag dolls than to name the puppy, so they skipped away. The boys settled down under a tree, taking turns petting the puppy as he sniffed around them.

"We want to be careful not to hurt Shep's feelings," Benjie said. "He is jealous of the puppy, but we want him to know we like him as much as ever." They looked around for Shep, but Shep had followed Dad out to the barn.

"Maybe Shep is in his second childhood," Nathan said. He settled himself more comfortably against the tree.

"Second childhood?" Benjie looked puzzled.

"It's like this," Nathan explained. "Take Aunt Mandy. She says and does things she would not have done when her mind was young. But when some people grow older they get mixed up. Some old people get childish in their minds. That is why they say 'in their second childhood.'"

"Well. Good old Shep doesn't act like a puppy. And he is still the best dog ever!" Benjie looked a little ruffled. No one was going to belittle Shep when he was around.

"Of course," Nathan agreed. He had to smile a little at Benjie's loyalty.

"Dad said he knew a man," Nathan continued, "who was always finding fault and criticizing other people when he was young. Now he is old and set in his ways. His children have a hard time taking care of him. Nothing suits him. He grumbles and complains about everything, even what they have to eat. If they have eggs for breakfast, he wants fried potatoes or cornmeal mush. Or he says the oatmeal is too salty or not salty enough."

Benjie listened closely. He was not allowed to complain about the food Mom fixed. "Maybe the old man did not have a father that learned him he should be thankful for every bite of food," Benjie said. "Dad says there are many poor people that would be glad if they could just eat the scraps we give to our dogs and cats."

"You mean taught," Ray corrected. "Don't you remember? Someone can teach you but not learn you. You have to do the learning, like this old man. He had to learn, and his father had to teach him."

Ray turned his attention back to Nathan. "Was the man an orphan? Or maybe he just never learned to be thankful."

"He must not have," Nathan agreed. "If a person tries to be thankful and to think kindly of everyone when he is young, then when he is old he will likely still be that way."

"I hope I don't grow into a grumbling, old

man." Benjie frowned thoughtfully. "I hope when my children are grown they will tell me if I am difficult to get along with."

Ray turned to look at Benjie's earnest face. Ray loved his younger brother, and he knew that sometimes Benjie took things very seriously and worried about them needlessly. Like the time when Benjie thought he had an incurable disease. There had been nothing wrong with Benjie at all!

"It is nothing to worry about, Benjie," Ray said kindly. "Let's just remember to be kind and thankful every day and that will take care of it."

Ray smiled. "And besides, if you ever have children they will probably be glad you are their father." Ray paused. Benjie was smiling too. He looked relieved.

"Just think about Shep," Ray said. "I don't think Shep will grow into a difficult old dog because he is always so good-natured.

"That is," Ray added hastily, "except toward the puppy. Shep needs time to get used to having another dog around. All these years he has been the only dog on the farm. We looked to him to do everything a dog should do."

Ray looked at the puppy, who was now stretched out on the grass, sleeping peacefully. "We still haven't thought up a good name for this little guy," he said.

"Hmmmm . . ." Nathan studied the sleeping puppy. "What about Skipper?"

"Skipper?" Ray said the word slowly, as if he were tasting it.

"Skipper?" Benjie's face lit up. "I like it! But he doesn't skip. Dogs don't."

"I know," Nathan nodded. "But Skipper means . . ." He looked at Ray for help. "A kind of ship, right?"

"It means the captain or master of a shipping vessel," Ray said. He looked thoughtful. "Who knows? The puppy might someday be kind of like a captain or master of dogs. Anyway, I like the name myself."

"Then Skipper it is!" said Benjie.

When Nathan and Alta got home, they could hardly talk fast enough. "Imagine our surprise," Nathan said, "when we walked into the kitchen and saw this strange man at Uncle David's table."

"Strange man?" Mother exclaimed. "What are you talking about?"

"Mother," Alta broke in, "he ate two whole pieces of pie, and Ellen said he often eats three whole pieces of bread if there is no pie, and he wants at least two cups of coffee at every meal, and he works for Uncle David!" Alta stopped for breath.

Eagerly Nathan went on, "He came and asked for a job, and Uncle David gave him one. He doesn't talk much, but he does good work. Ray said he has tried to strike up a conversation with him, but he is very close. He won't talk, except yes or no. We wonder if he is a spy."

Mother stood listening, openmouthed. "How does he look?" she asked. "Surely he is not a spy." She felt as though she had to investigate the man herself.

"His back is slightly bent, but he isn't humpbacked," Nathan explained eagerly. "He is real husky; stocky but not tall. He kind of shuffles as he walks. His clothes are old, but he looks fairly neat, for a tramp. He does not look like Tobias, the other tramp, at all. Tobias could not work like this man does. This man's name is Al. Al Camp."

Nathan paused to get a drink. "His name could be Alfred or Alvin, but all he said was Al."

Mother shook her head. "I am eager to see him myself," she admitted.

Then she thought of the thread. "Did Aunt Anna have thread that matched?" she asked.

Nathan and Alta stared at each other.

"Mother," Nathan stammered, "I-I clean forgot the thread. When Aunt Anna opened the door for us, the first thing we saw was Al Camp. And that was so exciting, I never once thought about thread."

"Neither did I," said Alta in a small voice. "And I especially wanted to bring home the thread for my new dress."

"Well, never mind." Mother glanced at the

clock. "I am fascinated by Al Camp too. I would likely have forgotten the thread myself. I'll just plan to sew another day."

Chapter 4

Another Surprise

One morning, while the Mast family was sitting around the breakfast table, their neighbor, Mr. Brown, drove in. Benjie jumped up and peered out the window. His eyes widened.

"Mr. Brown is getting out of his car with a box," he reported. "What could be in it? He carries it ever so carefully."

"Benjie, it is rude to stare out of the window," Mother reminded.

"Yes, come sit down," Dad said. He gave Toby a bite of sausage. Dad knew Mr. Brown was seldom in a hurry. They would all have time to finish eating breakfast.

Al sat holding the handle of his coffee cup and looking at it in the fondest way. Ray wondered, as he did so many times, what was going through Al's mind. If he was a spy, was he recording all that went on in the household? Or was he a harmless tramp, merely working as he moved from place to place? In some ways, he and the other tramp were the same. Neither one wanted to talk about himself, but Tobias had never eaten like Al did.

"I think his first bite goes into his big toe," Ellen had remarked one day. She had the idea that when you ate, you filled up your whole body.

At last everyone finished eating, and Al drank the last drops from his coffee cup. They all bowed their heads for silent prayer before leaving the table. Benjie bowed his head and thanked God for the good breakfast, but he was not thinking what he was praying. He was too busy wondering what Mr. Brown had in his box.

"What do you think he has?" Benjie asked almost before Dad lifted his head from prayer.

"I'm afraid, Benjie," Dad began kindly, "that your mind was on Mr. Brown instead of thanking God. I know how it is. Grown-ups have to guard their thoughts too. For instance, when a minister is preaching in church, before you know it your mind is wandering to other things. It is something we all need to work on. We need God's help to guide our thoughts."

Benjie hung his head. It was true. His mind had not been on God.

Al rose from his chair and left the room.

That was what he always did. As soon as they were done eating a meal, he would go to his room for a little bit. Was it to write something down? Was he keeping record of what they said and did? About ten minutes later he would be going out to do the work Dad had for him that day.

"I learned a poem when I went to school," Mom was saying. "The title was, 'Do I Really Pray?'" Mother glanced out the window to check on Mr. Brown. He was standing out at the garden and looking over it. He was holding the box very carefully. They knew he would knock when he was ready. Or maybe Dad would go out to meet him.

Dad looked out the window too. Then he picked up some dirty dishes and carried them over to the counter. "Maybe you could recite the poem for us," he encouraged Mom.

"Did the teacher learn it to you?" Benjie asked. He did not like to learn poems. In school, he was usually the last one to say his.

"She taught us the poem," Mom explained. "A teacher teaches you, remember? You are the one who learns."

"Doesn't a teacher learn anything?" Ellen wondered.

"Oh, yes," Ray spoke up. "Teachers learn things too. But you should say someone *taught you*. A teacher can teach you, or she can learn, but she can not learn you. You are the one that learns."

Benjie shook his head. He could not think about teaching and learning as long as Mr. Brown was walking around outside with a mysterious-looking box in his hands.

"We'll save Mom's poem for tonight," Dad said, picking up his hat. Benjie breathed a deep sigh of relief. He was fairly bursting with curiosity.

Dad stepped outside and met Mr. Brown, who was walking toward the house. Quickly Benjie and Ray followed Dad outside. Benjie hoped Mom wouldn't think he should stay and help Ellen with the dishes. He knew it was his turn.

I'll come and help Ellen as soon as I know what is in the box, Benjie thought to himself. He was very relieved when Mom didn't call him back.

For a few minutes Mr. Brown and Dad talked about the weather and the crops. Mr. Brown had noticed Al Camp when he passed by on the road, so Dad told him about Al. Ray and Benjie listened. It would not do to ask what was in the box, but they could hardly contain their curiosity. Mr. Brown held the box carefully. Every now and then it wobbled in his hands and tiny noises came out of it. *Why were grown-ups so slow?*

"This is rather suspenseful," Ray whispered. Benjie knew what that word meant, for Ray used it when something was about to happen but you didn't know what. It was an excited, wondering feeling.

Finally, when Benjie had almost given up hope, Mr. Brown said, "By the way, I wonder if the boys would be interested in taking care of these." He did not say what. He looked at the boys and smiled. Then he gently lowered the box and took off the cover.

Ray and Benjie peered eagerly into that box. Inside were four cute, little ducklings!

"One of my friends found a duck nest in the field where he was mowing hay," Mr. Brown explained. "The mother duck flew off, and my friend was afraid she wouldn't come back, so he brought the eggs over to us. We hatched them out with our incubator. Now the ducklings are getting too big to be in the house and are too little to turn loose."

"I imagine the boys would enjoy taking care of them," Dad said. He smiled at Ray and Benjie. He could tell how excited they were. "Would we have a pen for them somewhere?" he asked.

"Oh, yes!" Benjie said. He knew they could find *something* to keep the ducklings in.

"We could even make a pen," Ray said, already planning how he would build it.

"Very well," Dad chuckled. "We'll give it a try. But what do you boys say to Mr. Brown?"

Ray cleared his throat, and Benjie gulped. They had nearly forgotten their manners! "Thank you, Mr. Brown!" they said together.

After Mr. Brown left, Dad carried the box to the house, and they all gathered around to look at the little ducks.

"They will need a lot of water," Ray said. He looked around the kitchen. The only thing really big was Mom's washtub in the washhouse. He looked uncertainly at Mom. "Would it be suitable to use the washtub?"

"They don't need anything that big for now," Mom said. "Why don't you get the foot tub?" The foot tub was a bigger-than-usual pail. It was nice and round and roomy. The children used it when they washed their feet, so it was named rightly. But Mom used it in the garden, or anytime she needed a bigger pail.

Ray and Benjie hurried to find it, and fill it with cool water.

Carefully Dad gave Toby a little duck to hold.

"Don't squeeze it so hard," Mom said nervously. "You don't want to squash it."

The ducklings made little quacking noises, which sounded like they were trying to talk.

Ray and Benjie returned, carrying the full foot tub between them. Once in the water, the ducklings flapped their little wings joyfully. They flapped and splashed and dived under the water.

"Just think—their mother was not around to teach them how to swim!" Ellen said. She knelt beside the tub so she could watch every move

41

they made. The water splashed into her face, but she did not care.

"Isn't it marvelous?" Dad replied. "They know how to swim and dive, and no one taught them. What do we say the birds and animals have that helps them?"

"They have an instinct that tells them what to do," Ray answered quickly.

"That's right," Dad said. "We know God gave that instinct to the animals and birds. God made everything so right. Geese know when it is time to fly south. They don't make mistakes and fly north instead."

"And the purple martins know when it is time to leave," Benjie offered. "They don't hear us say it is time to go. They know already."

"And bears know when it is time to hibernate in the fall," Ray said. He thought a little more. "And squirrels know when to gather up nuts."

"We can't begin to think how wonderful God created everything," Dad said. He watched the ducks swimming and splashing happily in the water. "Just looking at those ducklings makes you feel that water is marvelous. You can see the ducks think so. And it is. We could not live long without water."

"Think of all the washing and cleaning we do!" Mom exclaimed. She looked at the unwashed breakfast dishes. "Suppose we had to haul all the water up from the creek."

"And what about the garden?" Ray asked. "I enjoy working in the garden. But without rain, nothing would grow."

"The crops would die," Benjie said. "And so would all the animals that drink water." Benjie had often seen Shep lapping up water. When Benjie fed the calves and gave them water, Shep would even come and drink water from the calves' pail.

Dad was glad the children were thinking. He wanted them to grow up appreciating God's wonderful blessings, and not taking them for granted.

"What about washing our hands?" Ellen said, wanting to put in her share.

"That reminds me," Ray said. "In deserts they wash their hands with sand. We learned that in our social studies class. The nomads never wasted water. It was so precious to them."

Benjie knew nomads in the desert moved around with their sheep and goats and camels to find grass or an oasis with water. Having to move often with one's flocks and herds, would be very different from what he was used to. Benjie wondered if the little nomad boys wished they did not have to move around like that. And they would not have soft beds to sleep in like he did. Likely they would wrap themselves in their camel-skin robes to sleep. Ray had told him all about the nomads.

"Well, I think we had better get to work," Dad said as he walked over to the door. "Ray, see if you can build a small pen for the ducks. Make it good and tight, so they can be out in the yard in it. As they grow, we can make a bigger pen."

Mom looked at Benjie. "Instead of helping with the dishes, you may help Ray," she said.

"Oh, Mom, thank you!" Benjie gave Mom a hug. How had Mom known how much he wanted to help Ray with the pen?

When Dad and the boys stepped outside, Shep was sitting there waiting for them. Skipper, the puppy, was frisking about Shep. He tried to stand on two legs and reach Shep's head. Then he fell over. He acted like Shep was a tree to climb. Shep just sat and looked down at Skipper. He looked as if he wondered what the puppy would try to do next. He was not frowning his dog frown. He even looked a little interested.

Dad and the boys praised Shep, and he wagged his tail. Eagerly Shep followed them to the barn, with the puppy scampering along, getting under their feet and making excited little barks.

"Shep is improving," Dad acknowledged.

"Maybe he will soon be friends with Skipper," Benjie said. That evening, as the family gathered in the living room for some quiet time, Mom recited the poem to them.

Do I Really Pray?

I often say my prayers,
But do I really pray?
And do the wishes of my heart
Go with the words I say?

I may as well kneel down
And worship gods of stone
As offer to the living God
A prayer of words alone.

For words without the heart
The Lord will never hear,
Nor will He to those lips attend
Whose prayer is not sincere.

Lord, show me what I need
And teach me how to pray,
And help me when I seek Thy grace
To mean the words I say.
—John Burton

Benjie looked very sober when Mom was finished. And Ray said, slowly, "I know I've prayed a lot of times when my mind was on other things."

"I try sometimes to say my night-time prayer as fast as I can," Benjie confessed. "I try to beat Ray to bed."

45

"Is that the way to pray?" Dad asked.

Benjie shook his head. "No, Dad."

"Suppose someone came and knocked at the door," Dad continued. "You would open the door, and the person would mumble something as fast as he could and then run away. It certainly would be rude, and it would not make you happy."

"No, it would not." Ray and Benjie shook their heads.

"I, for one, certainly want to do better," Ray said in his most grown-up voice.

"I would never want to pray to idols," Benjie stated. "And I do not want to act like the rude person who knocks and mumbles and runs away. I want God to know I love Him."

"Good," Dad said. "When we love someone, we love talking to him. So now you understand better, and I am glad Mom remembered the poem. You can be glad you learn poems in school."

Benjie nodded. Maybe someday he would recite the poems *he* learned in school, to his *own* children.

Chapter 5

Pepper

"**R**ay, you and Benjie may take this pipe over to Uncle Marks."

Dad looked at Ray to be sure he was listening. Just the mention of Uncle Marks made Ray and Benjie smile and sometimes forget what they were actually supposed to do.

"Take the pony cart," Dad was saying. "The pipe isn't long, but Uncle Mark needs it and the cart is the easiest way to take it."

"May we stay a while?" Benjie asked hopefully.

"If Mom doesn't need you, I don't care. Maybe a half hour or so."

Dad was barely finished talking before the boys hurried off to get the pony ready. They loved the pony. He was black with a white streak down his face. His name was Pepper, and it fitted him very well. If Pepper had been a very tame, gentle pony, they would hardly have liked him so well.

Pepper could act up and snort and gallop. He did not like to stand and wait. It made their rides so much more exciting to have a pony that was full of action. Pepper had strong likes and dislikes, but when he was in a good mood, he was a good pony.

"Now you be careful," Dad said as they started off. As usual, Pepper did not want to go away. In that respect he was lazy. It took some urging to get him started, and even then, he would try to turn around and head back. But once they were out the lane and onto the road, Pepper knew there was no use to protest. He plodded ahead.

Ray gave the lines a little slap. "He can be so poky," he said.

With a resigned air, Pepper increased his pace to a slow trot. "But other times he acts so feisty," Ray continued. "Just wait and see how he behaves on the way home."

"What does feisty mean?" Benjie asked. Benjie wished he knew all the words Ray knew, but he did not want to sit in the house reading to learn them.

"Why, it means full of nervous energy, or easily excited. That describes Pepper, doesn't it?" Ray replied.

48

"Not right now, it doesn't. He acts like an old plug."

"Just wait until we go home," Ray predicted.

As they passed Mr. Brown's house, his dog came out to the road and gave a bark or two. Pepper jumped and shied and started to gallop. Benjie held tightly to his hat. He and Ray were laughing. Sometimes the pony took no notice of the dog. It all depended on what mood he was in. Pepper was so little that he was easy to handle even if he tried to act like a wild horse.

When the boys passed Enos's home, they saw nothing of Enos. But Enos and his older brother Harvey saw them, for they were playing up in the hayloft. They saw the pony trying to gallop, fairly bouncing as he went.

"Enos, I have an idea," Harvey said.

"What is it?" Enos asked eagerly. He never knew what Harvey would think of.

"Let's show that pony some excitement on his way home," Harvey replied. Then he told Enos his plan.

Ray and Benjie left the pipe on Uncle Mark's porch. No one was at home at Uncle Mark's house, much to their disappointment. The door stood slightly ajar, and Benjie peered inside.

"I don't think they would mind if we got a drink and left a note," he said.

Ray looked thoughtful. "I know Aunt Ruth

would want us to make ourselves at home. Okay, we'll just get a drink."

The house seemed to echo with happy memories, but it was too quiet with no one there. Even the house seemed to be waiting until Uncle Marks came home.

"Feels like I have to see Nathan somewhere around here," Ray said.

Benjie was digging around in the trash can. "I'll write on the back of this old envelope," he said. He found a pencil on the bookshelf. Quickly he wrote,

> "We are terble sory no one is here. But we want to cum again. We brot the pipe for you and got a drink.
>
> Benjie"

Ray looked at the note. "You did not spell all the words right, but I suppose it will do. Let's go look at their goats, then we should go." They were careful to leave the house just as it was when they went in.

Benjie had an empty feeling. It just wasn't right being there and not seeing anyone. "Maybe they went to the dentist," he guessed. "Or maybe they are picking blackberries."

"Likely if we had walked here, we would have met them at the creek," Ray said.

Keturah, the mother goat, looked at the boys with a mild, curious expression on her face.

Goats were tricky. They could look innocent, as if they would never think of getting into mischief. But you could never trust a goat, for a goat *is* a goat. It naturally wants to climb and explore and eat almost anything. Keturah had had triplets, but one had died. Her two healthy kids were bumping each other around. They had to be penned inside while Uncle Marks were gone.

By this time Pepper was in a fine state of nerves. He neighed impatiently and jerked his head about. He pawed the ground. Why should he have to be standing here when he could just as well be in the pasture at home, eating grass? Sometimes it wasn't so bad, having to wait, but he had not been in the mood to go away this morning. Why were the boys so slow? Pepper could not talk, but his actions showed how he felt.

"You hold him until I can get on and hold the lines," Ray directed.

Benjie held Pepper's bridle. They weren't scared of Pepper, although he was rearing and trying to get loose. When Ray was settled on the cart, Benjie let go, made a dash for the cart, and leaped onto it. Pepper lost no time in starting off. Going home, he was like a different pony. No need to urge Pepper now. He started off at a gallop and the cart jostled and bounced out the lane. He acted as if he were running away, but the boys knew he was running for home. After a bit he settled down to a good trot.

As they neared Enos's home, Benjie looked around, trying to catch sight of his friend. But just then, from the ditch beside the road there rose a big, yellow canvas-coated figure. It looked like a walking ghost. It waved and flapped its arms.

"What is it?" Benjie gasped. Pepper took one look and bolted for the other side of the road. He leaped into the ditch, dragging the cart along. It lurched and tipped and almost overturned. Pepper bounded out of the ditch again and galloped furiously down the road, with the cart careening behind him. Benjie held his hat with one hand and clutched hold of the seat with the other. Ray, of course, was busy holding onto the lines.

When Ray and Benjie came dashing in the lane with Pepper, Dad came out of the barn. Pepper was snorting and puffing. "Boys, you should not make that pony run so fast when it is so warm," Dad said.

But when the boys told Dad what had happened, he looked rather grim.

"What those Yoder boys need is more work," Dad said, shaking his head. He examined the harness and the cart. Nothing was torn, and no one was hurt.

Then Dad went over the rules again. Even if there were few cars on the road, it was important to stay on the right side of the road. They must always look before crossing. Even though the pony was little, accidents could happen.

Meanwhile, Enos and Harvey were busy putting the big yellow canvas back in the corner of the hayloft. Every so often they had to stop and laugh. That surprised look on Ray's face! And Benjie's big eyes! And how that pony took off! Things had worked out just as Harvey had planned. If a car had been coming they would have had to give it up. But there was no traffic on the road—none except that little pony and cart with two boys in it. Harvey was sure he had never seen a pony take off so fast, though he had felt a little anxious when he saw how the cart lurched and almost overturned in the ditch.

Enos and Harvey did not feel so smart a few days later. Somehow or other, their father found out about their prank, and then he laid down some rules. One was, never scare a horse or pony on the road, no matter how little the pony is. Never play a trick that could hurt someone.

The evening after the prank, Dad talked to Ray and Benjie after he read the bedtime Bible story. Having been a boy himself, he knew it was fun to play tricks on your friends. "But," he warned, "never do anything that could hurt someone, in their body or their mind."

Seeing Benjie's puzzled expression, Dad went on to explain. Hiding a little boy's lunch box in school could make the little boy unhappy, and that would not be kind. Slipping a cookie into his lunch box, though, would be a nice little trick.

"It is much better to see what you can do to make someone happy," Dad said. "Never do anything that could scare a horse, or cause an accident. Many accidents could be prevented if people were more cautious on the road. And no matter what others do, remember you are responsible for your actions."

Ray nodded. He was glad nothing had happened, but he couldn't help thinking it had been rather exciting.

Benjie voiced what Ray was feeling. "But it was kind of fun, Dad."

"The next time it might not be," Dad said. "The cart could have overturned. You could have broken a leg, or hurt your head on the pavement. I know the Yoder boys did not stop to think, but let this be a lesson for you. Never do anything purposely that could hurt someone else. And," Dad went on, "Pepper is not as used to the road as he had been. The more we drive or ride him, the better."

Ray and Benjie nodded. They could take turns riding Pepper like they had when they first got him. Somehow the thrill of it had worn off, and they forgot about him, out in the pasture.

Chapter 6

Doing a Job Right

"It's my turn to feed the ducks!" Ray announced triumphantly.

Benjie glared at Ray. "No, it's my turn!"

"But you fed them last night," Ray objected. "Don't you remember?"

"Yes, but you took my turn yesterday morning."

"That was to even us up. I had to skip a turn before," Ray said.

"It wasn't my fault you had to skip a turn. I . . ."

"Now, boys—"

Ray and Benjie turned. They hadn't heard Dad coming. Dad didn't say anything more right away. He stood and looked at the little ducks. It was surprising how fast they grew. They were fed the same feed as the chicks, and every day they were given fresh water.

Dad was thinking. He had noticed that nearly every day, right after breakfast, Ray or Benjie would remember that the ducks needed to be fed.

"Well, go feed the ducks," Mom would say. She didn't want the ducklings to be out of food, and certainly not out of water. But the boy whose turn it was to feed the ducks forgot to come back in and do his share of the dishes. It was easier for Mom to finish the dishes herself than to call in a forgetful boy, who by this time was out in the barn or helping Dad.

Of course the boys checked the ducks in the evening too. They needed lots of water. Dad stroked his beard absently.

"I'm glad you take such an interest in the ducks, boys," he said. "But I want you to feed them before you come in for breakfast." Dad looked at Ray and then at Benjie. "You have a tendency of slipping out of your work in the house."

Benjie hung his head. How had Dad noticed?

Dad is awfully sharp, Ray thought. He felt ashamed of himself.

Mom had set up a system. Ray and Benjie and Ellen took turns with the dishes and housework. One morning it was Ray's turn to wash the dishes and Benjie's turn to wipe them. Ellen would clear off the table, scraping the crumbs into a scrap bowl. Then she wiped the table clean.

Ellen would also sweep the floor. The next time, it would be Benjie's turn to wash dishes, Ellen's turn to wipe them, and Ray's turn to clear the table and sweep the floor, and so on.

"I know you don't like washing dishes," Dad was saying, "but washing dishes never hurt anyone. It's not hard work. And it is good for us to learn to do jobs we don't like, and to do them well. Put your heart into whatever you have to do, and do your best."

"Dad, did you ever have to wash dishes?" Benjie asked.

"I had to wash dishes and more dishes."

"Did you like it?" Ray looked at Dad curiously.

Dad shook his head. "No, indeed! I'd poke around and poke around. So one morning my dad took me out to the washhouse and punished me. He told me any job worth doing is worth doing well. He said some people are so poor they would just be glad to *have* dishes to wash."

Benjie took a deep breath. It was a comfort knowing Dad had not liked the job either. *Washing dishes*, Benjie thought gloomily, *spoils my whole morning*. He listened carefully as Dad went on talking.

"After the punishment, I dug in and got the

57

dishes done in a hurry. It was a job I knew I had to do, and do well. It went better, because I stopped dreading it. I just pitched in and did it, and then I was finished."

"Breakfast is ready!" Ellen called from the kitchen door. "Mom said to hurry, or the pancakes will get cold."

"Pancakes!" Benjie exclaimed. He forgot all about washing dishes. He hurried inside with Ray and Dad to get washed up for breakfast.

Mom met them at the door. "I haven't seen Al yet this morning," she said. "Usually he sits on the porch swing until breakfast is prepared."

"I'll go see if he is ready," Dad said. "He would be sure to enjoy pancakes."

Dad soon came back. "He says he doesn't feel well this morning."

"I hope he is not getting sick," Mom worried. "Did you ask him if he wants something? Maybe a cup of hot tea to settle his stomach?"

"I didn't think to ask," Dad replied. "I'll just go and see if he would want some."

By the time Dad came back, the rest of the family was seated at the table waiting for him. "Poor Al," Ray was saying, "maybe he is getting homesick."

"How can he get homesick if he doesn't have a home?" Benjie asked.

Mom looked up as Dad came into the kitchen. "What does he want?" she asked.

"Why, he said . . ." There was a funny look on Dad's face. "He said a piece of cake or pie would be okay."

"What?! Cake or pie!" Mom exclaimed. She looked horrified. "And he says he isn't feeling well?" Mom took a deep breath. It was plain that Al Camp did not know how to eat when he was sick.

"Maybe he has an iron stomach," Ray said. They all had to laugh at that idea.

Mom shook her head. "Anyway, there is no cake around," she said, "and Al ate the last piece of pie yesterday."

"I wonder how Uncle Marks will manage when Al goes over there," Ray said. Uncle Mark had said he had some work for Al to do, especially as they prepared to host church services.

"I hope he will be feeling better by then," Mom said. She looked at Ellen. "When you set the table, you forgot to put on cups for the tea," she said. "Please get them now." Quickly Ellen fetched the tea cups from the cupboard.

"No tea for me," Benjie rhymed as Ellen set a cup beside his plate.

Ellen looked at Benjie. Her eyes widened in surprise. "Benjie! Your face is not clean," she said.

Everyone looked at Benjie. Mom smiled. "You were in too great a hurry, Benjie. Your arm isn't clean either. Use the washcloth and lots of soap," she advised. As Benjie hurried to the sink, he thought of Al Camp, and Tobias, the other tramp. Did anyone ever tell them their faces were dirty?

I think it would be rather nice being a tramp, Benjie thought. *Then I wouldn't have to keep washing my face all the time.*

A few minutes later, freshly scrubbed and finally clean, he walked back to join the others at the table. When he saw the circle of happy faces, he thought again about Al and Tobias.

They don't have a table full of family to wait for them, he thought. *Or to love them. I guess I'm glad I am not a tramp, after all.* He slid into his place on the bench, next to Ray.

They all enjoyed Mom's good breakfast. They felt sorry for Al, who was missing out on the pancakes. Al would have eaten an enormous stack of them.

"Maybe he'd enjoy some pancakes if we don't have any pie or cake to give him," Dad said, glancing at Mom. His eyes twinkled. He knew Mom would not give a sick person pancakes to eat, and most certainly not cake or pie.

"I have made more desserts since he is here!" Mom said, shaking her head. "He eats so much!"

"These pancakes make me think of Aunt Mandy," Dad said. He speared another one with his fork. Everyone remembered how much Aunt Mandy enjoyed Mom's pancakes.

"I wish she could visit us again," Benjie said sighing, "or we could visit her."

As the family left the table after breakfast, they heard Shep and Skipper start barking. Ray peered out the window. "They are barking at Engine," he said. The other children crowded to the window and looked out. When Skipper started barking at the cats, Shep would also give a bark or two.

It was surprising that Shep and the puppy had become good friends. Skipper would pull at Shep's tail and bark. When Shep sat down, Skipper would try to jump up to Shep's face. Shep would look down with an interested, friendly expression. In fact, it looked as though he were smiling his dog smile. He no longer showed his teeth.

"I am certainly glad those two are no longer at enmity with each other," Ray said in his most grown-up tone.

Benjie looked at Ray sharply. Sometimes he got tired of Ray's new words.

"It means like deep-seated hate between two people, or in this case it would be animals," Ray explained.

"The puppy didn't hate Shep," Benjie stated. He was rather glad that for once, Ray's new word did not fit.

"Benjie is right," Dad agreed. "There was no enmity on the pup's part." He was going to say more, but just then Mr. Brown drove in.

"So that's what the dogs were barking about!" Benjie said. He quickly turned from the window to rush outside, then stopped at the sight of the messy table. He was bursting to know what Mr. Brown wanted, but he knew it was his turn to wash the dishes. He glanced around the room. Couldn't he slip quietly outside? Dad was getting his hat, to go out. Ellen was wiping Toby's face and hands clean and pretending he was her baby. Ray started to clear off the table. Even though Mr. Brown was there, Ray remembered his goal to do better at his share of the work. And he knew the more quickly he did it, the sooner he could go outside.

Good old Ray, Benjie thought. *I don't want to make him do all the work by himself.*

Just then Ellen's voice cut into his thoughts. "It's your turn to wash the dishes, Benjie," she reminded.

"Mom, Ellen doesn't give me a minute's peace," Benjie said, frowning. He had been ready to pitch in and work fast, but he did not like to be reminded all the time by his little sister.

Mom knew how Benjie felt, but she also knew Ellen was pretending. "Ellen likes to pretend you are her little boy," Mom explained, smiling at Benjie. "I suppose it is human nature that does not like to be told what to do. I remember when I was little, we children liked to surprise our parents and do things without being told. But we also needed to take orders—and do the work we were told to do.

"We used to race with the clock," Mom went on. "We would try to be done in fifteen minutes, and how we would hurry! It is surprising how much you can do even in five minutes when you try."

Quickly Benjie got out the dishpans and set to work. "I'd like to race too." Then Ellen and he worked so fast that it was fun. They were almost breathless by the time they were finished.

"You did it right," Mom said, "and now you may go out to Dad and Mr. Brown."

Chapter 7

The School of Life

When Mr. Brown came over that morning, he had brought along an oblong tub he had found at the flea market. He brought it for the ducks. Ray and Benjie filled it with water and let the ducks out of their pen.

"Ducks are cautious creatures," Mr. Brown observed, nodding toward the little ducklings. He walked over to a tree and leaned against it. Mr. Brown was in no hurry to go. He wanted to see the ducks dive around in his tub.

Later, Ray and Benjie worked in the garden and let the ducks out of their pen for awhile. The ducklings loved to be free. They flapped their little wings and made contented duck noises. They seemed to be talking together. They followed Ray and Benjie to the garden, waddling along in single file. They found bugs and insects under leaves of plants, and with their bills they spooned around in the dirt.

Mom had decided she liked ducks in the garden. They did not hurt the plants. The ducks did not scritch-scratch like chickens do, or take dust baths. No, ducks were different. With their webbed feet they waddled around gently between the plants.

"Maybe big, tame ducks would be different if they were in a garden," Mom said. "But these little, wild ducks do no harm at all."

What the ducks liked best was water. Oh, how they loved the water! Just watching them made you marvel at the wonder of water. When it rained, Ray or Benjie would let the ducks out of their pen. Watching them made Benjie wish he were a duck too.

The ducks made happy noises as they talked together. As the rain dropped from the roof in puddles, the ducks dipped their bills into the ground until they had made little mud holes. The ducks liked nothing better than to spoon up the mud and then dip their bills into the water again.

But there were no mud holes around when it didn't rain. So now the boys filled the tub with water. You'd think the ducks would jump in right away, but as Mr. Brown said, ducks are cautious. They did not know what this tub was, and they did not even come close to it. Benjie caught a duck and put it into the tub. Just as quickly, the duck jumped out. Once it was out, however, the duck realized it had been in water. In no time at all, it was waddling around trying to get back in.

Mr. Brown laughed. "It wants back in, but it doesn't know enough to jump up."

Ray put a flat stone in front of the tub. It took some time, but after a while the duck caught on and used the stone as a step to get into the tub. Then what a splashing there was! The duck spread out its wings and tried to dive under the water. By this time the other three ducks wanted to get into the tub too.

The next duck to get in went after the first duck and chased it out. Then two more ducks jumped in. There was so much splashing that soon the tub was half empty.

"Pretty soon they will be big enough to take care of themselves," Mr. Brown said, straightening up to go. "Then they will start flying."

He nodded wisely. "When they are able to fly, you will want to take them to the creek and set them free."

"Some people clip ducks' wings so they won't fly away," Ray said, "but I wouldn't want to do that."

"I agree with you," Mr. Brown said. He paused and looked at the ducks again. "They were born to be free. It's their wild nature. They aren't like tame ducks."

Mr. Brown smiled at the boys. "But they are

your ducks now, so you do what you want with them. I know you will be good to them."

"I hope they don't fly for a long, long time," Benjie said after Mr. Brown left. "I don't want the ducks to leave us."

"They learn to fly, and we learn to work," Ray said. He picked up the pail to get more water. "But I wish they would want to stay." Ray loved the ducks too.

On Thursday, Dad took Al Camp over to Uncle Mark's farm. Al had not stayed sick very long. Mom felt he had simply been eating too much cake and pie. He did not eat many vegetables. He always took a helping of whatever Mom made, but it was plain that bread and desserts were his main foods.

At the dinner table, Dad told the children about the new plans for the school term. Instead of going to the school they went to last year, they would attend the Meadow Brook School. Ray listened with an eager expression on his face, but Benjie gave a great sigh. He did not want to think about school—much less a different school.

"What will make it more interesting," Dad said, "is the new family that moved into the other district. They have a deaf girl, so you will be learning sign language. Your teacher will be Abe Graber."

"Sign language!" Benjie echoed. "You mean I would talk with my hands?" Benjie laid down his fork and looked at his hands. He had seen some people in the dentist's waiting room, talking sign language. Their fingers seemed to fly as they motioned and made all sorts of signs, and then they would laugh and act as if they knew exactly what the other person was signing.

Benjie was sure he would never be able to learn sign language. Going back to school did not give him a happy feeling either.

"Now, Benjie," Dad was saying, "you have learned to read in school, and to get along with others. School is all about learning new things. In a way, we are all still in school. We never stop learning in the school of life." Dad looked at Benjie's long face. He wanted Benjie to look on the bright side.

"You enjoyed going to school last year, didn't you, Benjie?" he asked.

Benjie stopped to think. Now that he thought of the children, and the teacher, and the good times they had had—yes, he knew he had enjoyed it. Then he thought of how he felt now.

"I enjoyed it," Benjie said slowly, thinking, "but now I enjoy the summer so much more that I don't want to think of anything else."

"I think you will find it interesting," Dad encouraged. "Think about it—a new school, a different teacher . . . and you will be walking to school, going north instead of west."

Dad helped himself to more green beans and

passed them to Benjie. Benjie's mind was not on eating. Without thinking he took a huge second serving of beans.

"Dad, will Enos be going to Meadow Brook School too?" Benjie asked.

"I don't know yet, Benjie. It depends on the number of children each school will have."

Benjie thought about that. His first thought was that he would be glad if Enos were not in his school. Enos would not be there to tease and torment him. Then Benjie remembered the time he was sick with chicken pox. When he returned to school, Enos was glad to see him again. Enos made him feel welcome. He thought of all the good times he and Enos had had together. Sometimes Enos was a good friend. Sometimes he was not.

"Wouldn't you miss Enos if he weren't in school?" Dad asked.

"Yes," Benjie said. "I know I would miss him. Enos is my dear enemy."

Mom and Dad's faces were puzzled, and Benjie hastened to explain. "Sometimes he is a good friend, and sometimes I can hardly like him. He plays mean tricks and things."

"Well, try to think of him as your friend," Dad advised. "It is all a part of growing up. It's one of those hard lessons in the school of life: learning to get along with our fellow men. We need to be kind and forgiving. If everyone treated us nicely and just as we wanted to be treated, we would not learn to be forgiving and forbearing." Dad studied Benjie's face. He was not sure Benjie understood what he meant.

"Take the animals," Dad said. "They cannot reason and think as people do. They follow their instincts and do as God created them to do. But God gave people the ability to think and make choices. The animals don't know the Golden Rule. When you feed the calves, they push and shove, and each one wants to be first."

Benjie nodded. The calves acted so greedy. "But sometimes Enos pushes and shoves too," he said. "He always wants to be first to get a drink." Benjie took a bite of beans without noticing what he was eating.

"There is your chance to put into practice the Golden Rule," Dad replied. "What would you think if Uncle Mark and I each tried to be first to use the corn planter, or if he would take more than his share of hay? In the school of life we learn to share and to be honest and unselfish. No matter how others treat you, always remember it is how *you* treat *them* that counts. Jesus loved those who were mean to Him, and He taught His followers to love even their enemies. The more we learn to love Jesus, the more we will be able to love those who treat us unkindly."

Ray and Benjie were listening carefully.

Ray knew he wanted to try harder than ever to

be the kind of boy Dad and Mom wanted him to be. "We should not boast either, should we?" he asked suddenly.

"No, we shouldn't," Dad replied. "All we have comes from God. If we can do anything well, it is because God gave us the ability and strength to do it."

Ray looked down at his plate. He knew, deep down, that sometimes he felt wise and smart because he read a lot and knew so many words.

That afternoon when Ray and Dad were alone in the barn, Ray told Dad how he felt. "I don't want to feel I am smart, but the feeling just comes," Ray admitted.

Dad did not say anything right away. He looked very thoughtful. "It is so easy to have a feeling of pride in our hearts," Dad began slowly, "but pride is one of the things God hates."

"Yes," Ray said, hanging his head.

Dad laid his hand on Ray's shoulder. "Honestly, I don't think you want to be proud about what you know," he said kindly. "If you feel that self-satisfied feeling creeping into your heart, just tell God about it. Ask Him to help you remember that He gave you your reasoning, and your ability to think and learn. Thank Him for giving you a sound mind, and ask Him to help you use it always to His honor and glory."

Dad smiled at Ray. "I am glad you told me this. It helps to share things and talk them over. I hope whenever you have questions or temptations you will want to tell me about them."

Ray swallowed hard. Dad was so kind and strong and gentle. "I hope someday I can be just like you," he blurted.

"That makes me happy, Ray. But I, too, have faults. If we make Jesus our example and live for Him, we will not go wrong." Dad pulled out his handkerchief and blew his nose. Nothing made him happier than to know that his children wanted to do what was right. And it was true, as a minister had preached once: There was nothing on earth that a man could take to heaven, except his children.

On Sunday the church services were at Uncle Mark's home. Several times before, Dad had invited Al to go along with them to church, but he always had an excuse. But now, since he was helping Uncle Marks, he was there. Ray and Benjie had to smile when they saw Al sitting beside Uncle Mark in church. Al could understand German, and he spoke Pennsylvania Dutch just like the rest of them.

Of course people wondered who he was. He wore clean everyday clothes. He did not talk unless someone talked to him. After lunch, of which he ate a goodly amount, he retired to his room.

"How did you get along with Al?" Mom asked Aunt Ruth, as she collected her wraps to go home.

Aunt Ruth rolled her eyes. "Maybe you should ask him how he got along with us. Friday, at dinner, I told him we didn't have any dessert. Then he said, 'Didn't the hired girl have time to make cake or pie?' " Aunt Ruth and Mom had to laugh but they both looked rather exasperated.

"He should eat more tomatoes and lettuce and other vegetables," Aunt Ruth said. "But he wants his bread and pastries and his coffee. And have you noticed how he sits and looks at his coffee cup? He looks at that cup as if it were the most important thing around."

"He loves his coffee," Mom agreed. "He is the most unusual tramp I've ever met."

"Yes, and Nathan has come to the conclusion that he is a harmless one," Aunt Ruth returned.

"I think he was hoping Al was a spy or a detective. The boys have had such ideas about him. But Al does have some surprising habits. The next time he sits on your porch swing, watch him." Aunt Ruth looked mysterious.

"Now what could he be doing sitting harmlessly on the swing?" Mom wondered.

But Aunt Ruth would not say another word, except "Just watch once."

As Mom was going out to the buggy, Enos's

mother called after her. "Don't forget about the sign language class Friday evening at Meadow Brook School."

"Is it for everyone?" Mom asked.

"Everyone who cares to come. But of course we hope the school children especially will be there. The teacher decided to have some classes before school starts. It will be so much nicer for Elizabeth, if the children can talk to her in sign language."

Elizabeth was the girl who could not hear. She could not hear the birds sing. She could not hear the rain drumming on the roof. If she wanted to cross the road, she could not hear whether a car was coming. She could not hear a baby cooing and laughing. She could not hear her mother's comforting voice. She lived in a silent world. Even so, God loved Elizabeth, and He had a purpose and plan for her life.

Chapter 8

Chiggers

There Mom was! Benjie had looked for her everywhere. Finally he'd found her in the coat closet, straightening things up. Wraps had fallen on the floor. Several coats hung there which were not needed in warm weather. Mom did not like a clutter in the closets. She wanted every closet in good order.

"Mom, I have to scratch and scratch!" Benjie groaned.

Mom turned and looked keenly at her son. "What is the matter, Benjie?" she asked. "Did you get poison ivy somewhere?" Mom knew how well Benjie liked to explore. When Benjie was in the woods, he didn't think about watching out for poison ivy.

"Let me look once," Mom said. She pulled up his shirt and examined his middle. Yes, there were welts all around his waist, but they did not look like poison ivy.

Ray and Ellen had followed Benjie into the house, curious to hear what Mom would say about his itchiness. The three children had been playing hide and seek outside on this beautiful Tuesday morning. But Benjie grew so uncomfortable that he had finally stopped the game and gone looking for his mother.

"Mom," Ray spoke up, "on Sunday we went back to the woods and Benjie and Rob. . . ."

"Just a minute," Mom interrupted. "Who is Rob?"

Ray started it again. "Why he is one of. . . ."

Then Ellen spoke up. "He is Becky's brother. Becky is nice. She played with us, and she is a friend to the deaf girl."

"Oh," and Mom nodded. "You mean the new family that moved in several months ago. Yes, it was nice seeing them in church, but I didn't know they have a Rob in their family."

"Well," Ray began again, patiently, "he and Benjie walked way back into the deep part of the woods."

Mom's face grew serious. She was thinking of snakes, and of her son getting lost deep in the woods. "Next time, Benjie, you stay with Ray and the other boys," Mom instructed.

"Yes, Mom," Benjie said, scratching harder than ever.

Suddenly a look of relief came over Mom's face. "Benjie, you have chiggers!" she exclaimed. "I feel certain that is what it is. Chiggers are usually in woods or fence rows that are grown up with weeds." Mom drew a deep breath. She was glad to know it wasn't poison ivy.

"Chiggers!" Benjie exclaimed. He looked distastefully at his bites. He had heard of chiggers before, but he didn't actually know what they were. "How come they jumped on me?" he asked.

"Listen, Benjie," Ray said, eager to explain. "Chiggers are found in places where it is more wild and uninhabited by people."

Benjie looked puzzled. "What is unhabited?"

"The word is un-in-hab-it-ed." Ray pronounced the word slowly. "It means places where people don't generally go. Chiggers are tiny mites. So tiny you can't see them."

Benjie peered down at his bites. There was a big one on his ankle. Surely if he looked hard enough he would be able to see a chigger there.

Ray shook his head. "You won't be able to see them no matter how hard you look."

"They get into your skin and cause severe itching," Mom said. "I don't know how long they last. Maybe a week or more. I used to get them when I picked wild blackberries."

"Do you think they will last until Friday?" Benjie asked hopefully.

77

Mom and Ray looked surprised.

"You sound as if you like them!" Ray exclaimed.

Benjie bent down to scratch his ankle again. "Well, I can't go to sign language class Friday evening. I can't sign 'cause I will be too busy scratching," Benjie stated.

Mom sat down and began to laugh. "Benjie, surely it is not that bad. Just think. None of the children know how to speak sign language. No one will notice if you make mistakes." Mom gave Benjie's shoulder a pat. "Dad will take you and Ray and Ellen. Maybe he will stay for the class too."

Benjie thought about that. With Dad there, it would be different. No, it would not be so bad after all. Not with Dad there. Benjie stopped to think about how it was for children who had no father. For a little he forgot his chiggers.

No matter what his trouble might be, Dad always knew how to help him. Dad was strong and safe and right. Even if Dad were a cripple, he would be strong inside.

Benjie took a deep breath. Then he looked at Mom. Of course there was no one like Mom, either! When he was sick, it was Mom he wanted. It was Mom who comforted him and knew just how to make him feel better. How many times had Dad and Mom helped him when he was troubled!

"Benjie," Mom was saying, "about the only thing that kills chiggers is putting clear fingernail polish on the bites. But we don't have anything like that in the house."

Mom led Benjie into the bathroom. She put rubbing alcohol on his bites. In fact, she went through the medicine cabinet. Anything she thought would help the itching, she put on Benjie's bites.

"That burns," Benjie said, as Mom dabbed yet something else on a bite. "But it feels good too."

"I don't think this will kill them," Mom said, "but maybe it will relieve the itching a bit."

"I wonder how God could think of chiggers when he made the earth," Benjie said.

Mom put the cap back on the bottle. "We cannot begin to imagine how great and marvelous God is, Benjie. It is too deep for us to understand. And we know God's love for us is so wonderful, that even though there is much we do not understand, we can still trust Him and love Him. God has a wise reason for everything. We are reminded often of God's wisdom in comparison to our lack of understanding."

When Benjie went back outside, he found Ray waiting for him. Ray sniffed the air. "You smell like a walking medicine cabinet, Benjie," he said, grinning.

Chapter 9

Showing Compassion

The next day, Uncle Mark brought Al Camp back. By next week Dad would be finished with Al. In fact he could have sent him on now, but he felt Al would rather set off at the beginning of the week. Also, Dad wanted Al to know ahead of time so he could plan where he wanted to go next.

That night they had watermelon for supper. Al liked watermelon. He put both salt and pepper on it. Al put so much black pepper on his watermelon that he had to sneeze. The children looked at Al wonderingly. His watermelon was covered with black pepper. Mom had read somewhere that pepper is hard on our heart, so the children were not to use much. Now Al sneezed several times. He used a lot of salt and pepper on all his food, even though Mom had already seasoned it so that it tasted just right.

"Maybe he is so old and tough that black pepper doesn't hurt his heart," Ray remarked that evening, as the family sat together in the living room.

"Red pepper is said to be good for you," Mom said. But Al did not use red pepper. Mom wished she could do more for Al. She tried to make him feel at home, but she didn't know what else she could do.

Ray and Benjie liked Al, but they could not make friends with him as they could with Tobias, the other tramp. "I wonder why he doesn't talk more to us," Benjie said. "I would like him to think I am his friend. How can I count him as a friend if he doesn't act like one?"

Dad looked thoughtfully at Benjie, and tried to explain. "We can't tell how Al feels inside. Do you know what *compassion* means, Benjie?"

"Not exactly," Benjie replied doubtfully.

"It means to feel sorrow or pity for other people's troubles—to be tender, kind, and merciful to others. If you have compassion for others, you care about them. Being able to have compassion for others, even if you don't know them well— that is the main thing. Likely, Al never had much of a home. Maybe he never had parents to teach him."

Dad pulled absently at his beard. Benjie was listening. He knew Dad was thinking what to say next. Benjie liked when Dad talked to him like this.

Finally Dad spoke. "The Bible says, 'A man that hath friends must shew himself friendly.' If you live to be old, you will meet a lot of people. Naturally, you will not be able to have everyone for a friend. Not a close friend. But you can always be friendly and care enough to show compassion. It means when you are in a hurry going somewhere and someone needs help on the way, you will take time to help him."

"Like the Good Samaritan?" Benjie asked.

"That is right. That is a fine example of compassion. He cared about the man who was hurt and was a neighbor to him. You can't say the hurt man was his friend at the time, but maybe afterwards. Who knows? Maybe they became friends."

"I hope they did," Benjie said. He liked to imagine the Good Samaritan coming back to the inn and talking to the hurt man.

"So even if Al does not seem responsive and want to talk," Dad concluded, "you can still think of him as a friend."

"I *will* count him as a friend, even if he doesn't seem like one," Benjie said, smiling. "I can have old friends and young friends and little friends and big friends. And compassion for all the people I meet."

"That is right!" Dad looked pleased. "It doesn't matter how people treat you. The important thing is how you treat them."

Ray had been listening quietly as Dad and Benjie talked. He was old enough to think about Dad's example, not just his words. Ray knew that Dad was compassionate toward others. Dad was a good example for Ray and Benjie to follow.

Even though Al was not talkative, Dad would visit with him at the table and try to make him feel at home. Uppermost in Dad's mind was the concern that Al Camp had peace with God.

When they had family devotions in the morning, Al would listen quietly while they read the Bible. He would kneel down to pray when they did, but he did not take part in worship.

"There are many things I could say to Al," Dad said, "but if we do not live our faith, all our words are meaningless. A man preaches a louder sermon by his walk of life than by any eloquent words he says."

* * * * *

The next day it rained, and it was too wet to do much outside. What could they give Al to do?

"I have some nuts he could pick out of the shells," Mom suggested. "I don't have time to get it done myself."

At first Al did not look very happy about picking out nutmeats.

"I want to make a nut pie," Mom explained.

Al perked up. "A pie? How much sugar goes into a nut pie?" Al asked.

"Nut pie takes more than some pies," Mom replied. "I'm not sure how much exactly."

Al's face brightened. He smiled his slow smile, and set to work with a will. Mom knew she wouldn't get the pie made in time for Sunday, but she would try to make it early in the next week.

Sunday morning when Mom came into the kitchen, she was startled to see Al sitting at the table picking out more nutmeats. She gasped in surprise. She had set the nuts on the shelf, but Al had seen where they were.

"Oh, we don't want you to do that on Sunday!" Mom exclaimed. "You know, Sunday is the Lord's Day, and we don't want to do any unnecessary work on Sunday." She looked at the pan of nutmeats. "I can see you already have enough for a pie."

Soon Dad and the boys came in from doing the chores. Turning to Al, Dad said, "Al, we would be glad if you would go with us to church today."

Al sat deep in thought. "Well," he said after a bit, "I think I will go along today." He nodded and smiled a little.

Everyone was glad to hear that. They did not like to go to church and leave Al at home alone. It was very important to go to church and worship God and listen to the sermons and help sing.

* * * * *

The next week Mom made a nut pie. The way Al Camp smiled, they knew he enjoyed it. That evening he sat on the porch swing.

No one ever stopped to watch when Al was sitting there. But now Mom remembered what Aunt Ruth had said.

Al swung slowly back and forth. Then suddenly Al spat across the porch into the yard. Mom looked at Al again. Al had a great big wad in the side of his cheek.

"He is chewing tobacco!" Mom gasped. Dad, who had been sitting at his desk, came to the window. He was just in time to see Al spit again.

"All the time he has been here, we have never noticed," Mom said. "I am glad he is leaving. I would not want the children to pick up such a dirty habit."

When Al left the Masts' place, he stayed in the community for a while longer. Some other families had work for him, so he went from place to place until there was no more work for him to do.

Mom's heart went out to Al. What enjoyment did he get out of life except eating? What purpose or aim did he have? What happened in his early years that he had chosen a hobo's life? Only God would ever know the state of Al Camp's heart.

Chapter 10

Adjusting to Changes

Ray and Benjie were sorry to see Al Camp leave. Having him around gave their farm an interesting air, for there was always the hope that something exciting would turn up with Al.

"And we are his friends even if he doesn't know it," Benjie stated. "He doesn't seem to care, one way or the other."

"But we never got to peep into his satchel," he added regretfully. "I almost asked him if I could peek inside, but I didn't."

"It would have been very rude," Ray said. "You should never ask to look into people's suitcases. We should not be nosy."

The boys were tending the ducks as they talked. Carefully Ray opened the pen, and the four ducks came waddling out. Then it happened. One of them spread its wings and suddenly rose

87

into the air. Up, up it flew, over the barn and away, until it was only a small speck high in the sky. The other ducks did not seem to notice. They splashed around in their tub and quacked contentedly.

"I don't want them to fly away," Benjie said, still gazing up into the sky.

"I know," Ray agreed, soberly. "But like Mr. Brown said, they were born to be free."

Shep came sniffing around the pen, but the ducks were not afraid of Shep.

As the boys were putting the ducks into the pen, they heard the noise of flapping wings. Looking up, they saw the duck was circling overhead. It landed clumsily in the garden and came waddling back to the other ducks.

"Hooray!" Benjie cheered.

But they could not keep the ducklings for long. The next morning all *four* ducks took off into the sky. They did not come back until after dinner.

"It's time to take them down to the creek," Dad said. "They are not happy in that pen."

So the next morning Ray and Benjie took the ducks down to the creek. When the ducks saw all that running water, they were as happy as ducks can be! Eagerly they plunged into the water, where they splashed and dived and spooned into the bottom. O how they loved that sparkling, cold, wonderful water!

Ray and Benjie could not feel very sad when they saw how glad the ducks were to be there. After watching them for a little while, the boys trudged on home.

But the next morning the ducks returned. Hungrily they gobbled the feed that was still in a hopper outside their pen. During the next week the ducks came and went as they pleased.

Then one day only three ducks returned, and finally, none came.

"Do you think something got them?" Ray asked.

Dad shook his head slowly. "It could be," he said. "Maybe we made a mistake. They were not afraid of Shep, so likely they would not have been afraid of a fox either."

Dad thought about the ducks. "Their duck mother would have taught them to fear the dogs, and it would have been for their good. I didn't stop to think that we were not teaching them how to take care of themselves in the wild. Yet there is no telling. Maybe they are doing just fine on their own. But next time we have something wild, we want to let it keep its fear of the dogs."

"We were not fair to them, were we?" Ray asked as he soberly took down the ducks' pen. Benjie picked up the feed hopper. The boys wanted to think their ducks were somewhere in the wild, enjoying the creek and living the life of wild ducks. But it would have been so easy for a fox to nab them and gobble them up. The unsuspecting ducks would likely have thought the fox was just another dog, like Shep.

Inside the house, in the kitchen, Dad and Mom were talking in undertones.

"Why don't we tell the boys now?" Mom was saying. "It would give them something to look forward to. I know they are feeling unhappy about the ducks."

When Ray and Benjie came into the house, Dad motioned them over.

"We have a surprise for you," Dad said. He looked at Mom. "Why don't you tell them?"

The boys looked at Dad and then at Mom. Both parents were smiling. Benjie took a deep, excited breath. *What can it be? Are we going over to Uncle Marks? Is Mom planning a picnic? Are Uncle Marks coming over for supper? Is Dad getting a new horse?* So many ideas tumbled through Benjie's mind.

Then Mom spoke. Her voice sounded excited. "We are getting company," she said. "Someone special is coming to stay with us for a while."

Benjie's mouth dropped open in surprise. What could be better than that?

"To stay with us!" Ray exclaimed. "Who—"

"Someone special?" Benjie interrupted. He stared open-mouthed at Mom. "Who is it? Is it Grandpas? Is it Aunt Mandy? Who is it, Mom?"

"Now Benjie, you talk so fast. Wait and we

will explain," Dad said. "Uncle Alberts are bringing my cousin Danny."

"Is he our age?" Ray asked hopefully.

"No, he isn't," Dad said, shaking his head. "He is in his thirties, I would say."

Ray's face fell. He had already been picturing Danny as a boy his age.

"You have never seen Danny," Dad explained. "He is Uncle Albert's stepson's boy. His parents are not well. So the kinfolks are taking turns caring for Danny."

"But why doesn't he take care of himself?" Benjie wondered. "Is he a lazy man?" He looked at Ray, puzzled. He could see that Ray, who was usually quite wise, did not understand either. A man, in his thirties already, not able to take care of himself?

"Danny is different," Dad explained carefully. "Danny will always have the mind of a child. He has Down syndrome."

"Oh," Ray nodded, "I see. Those children are special, aren't they?"

"Yes," Dad answered, "they are. Remember, we are all special to God. But these children are special in that they are always innocent. Their minds do not develop like yours."

Dad was still talking. "So, even though Danny is much older than you, he will be more like a child than a grown man. He will be staying with us for about six weeks."

Benjie tried to imagine how it would be to have Danny there for six weeks. There was no telling what all they might do together!

"I wonder why Down syndrome children are the way they are," Ray pondered. "I read somewhere that they are usually cheerful and loving, but they don't grow big."

"That is right," Dad said, nodding. "I read up on this since I found out Danny is coming. Down syndrome children are described as lively and lovable. You will not understand what this is, but a normal person has 46 chromosomes, whereas the Down syndrome child has 47. One too many."

"And that is what causes it?" Mom shook her head in wonder.

"Mankind is fearfully and wonderfully made," Dad said. "We know God makes no mistakes. There is a reason for these very special children." Dad smiled at the boys. "I know you will want to make Danny's stay a happy one."

"I couldn't really be friends with Al Camp," Benjie mused. "But now I can have Danny for a friend."

"Indeed you can," Mom agreed. "But remember, you can still think of Al as a friend, even though he didn't seem friendly. It is hard for some people to open up. If children grow up without loving, caring parents, it is harder for them to be friendly; for they never learned how."

Benjie thought about that. He tried to imagine how it would be if Dad and Mom were not friendly. Suppose, when Mr. Brown came over, Dad would not smile and talk to him. Ray was thinking the same thoughts, only he was thinking about Mom.

"I'm so glad you are always friendly and kind," Ray said, looking at Mom. "Do you remember the other Sunday when those new folks were in church?" Ray paused, and Mom nodded to show she remembered.

"Well, one of my friends said he wished his folks would invite them over, 'cause he likes when they have company. But he said his mom doesn't like to have company if she doesn't know it ahead of time."

"Oh, yes!" Benjie cut in eagerly. He had heard the conversation too. "And you know what Sammy said to him?"

"Sammy talks slowly, but he gets it said," Ray put in.

"Now, boys," Dad reproved, "you should not interrupt each other. It is being kind and polite to let the other person go on and say what he started to say." Ray and Benjie looked at each other.

"You say it, Ray."

"No, you say it, Benjie."

Dad smiled. "You started it, Ray."

"Well, Sammy said his mother said that Mom,

he meant our mom, is the most hospitable person around. No matter if it's unexpected, Mom always invites strangers."

Benjie beamed at Mom. It gave him a good feeling to know people noticed how kind Mom was. He knew what *hospitable* meant. It meant being kind and warm-hearted and generous. Ray had explained it to him as they walked home from church.

"Why . . . why . . ." Mom stammered, blushing and looking a little flustered. "I know I'm no more so than others. But I always have to think, 'Suppose we were strangers somewhere and no one would notice us?' Besides, I love to have company. And boys," Mom looked serious now, "I want you to know as you grow up, if there is a visitor in the group, always invite him."

"Yes," Dad nodded. "We want you to know that you are always welcome to bring your friends home. Friends or strangers."

"I know so often the house should be cleaner and the windows washed," Mom went on. "And I don't always have something baked on hand. But I don't want those things to keep me from having company."

Benjie was thinking. "The Bible doesn't say you have to have a clean house before you have company, does it?" he asked.

"No, it doesn't," Dad agreed heartily. "But it does encourage us to open our home gladly to others." Dad shook his head. "No, the Bible says nothing about having cake or pie on hand, or having the windows washed; but we are admonished to practice hospitality without grudging."

"And now if Danny comes we will be hospitality to him," Benjie said happily.

"We'll be hospitable," Mom corrected gently.

"And I think Danny will fit right in," Dad said. "You will find there are things he cannot do. But he will be another friend, and the more friends we have, the richer we will be."

Chapter 11

Cleaning the Feed Room

The next week everyone hustled around getting ready for the company.

"I need you boys to clean out the feed room today," Dad said at breakfast. "It should have been done sooner."

Dad passed the platter of eggs to Benjie, who looked at Mom. "Did you make me two?" he asked.

"I made two for you and two for Ray and two for Dad," Mom answered. She was thankful the hens were laying so well. Eggs could be prepared so many different ways and still be good. Sometimes she fried them; sometimes she served poached eggs. Or scrambled eggs. Or omelet.

This morning Mom had sliced potatoes and fried them lightly. The potatoes and poached eggs were a fine breakfast. When tomatoes came in season, they would have sliced tomatoes too.

The day before, Mom had made fruit bars. They were somewhat like a sponge cake but made on a cookie sheet, because they were bars instead of cake. Then Mom spread a fruit filling on top. This time Mom used apple pie filling, but any kind of fruit filling was good. When the bars were baked and out of the oven, she put a lemon glaze over them.

Remembering that they could eat the delicious bars with their cereal, Benjie did not waste any time. He started right in on his eggs.

"Mom," Ray said, looking around the table, "Where is the applesauce?" Ray especially liked applesauce with his eggs and potatoes.

"Oh, I forgot the applesauce. Do you want to get a jar?" Mom asked.

Ray nodded. It was no trouble going to the cellar for a jar of Mom's good applesauce.

Right after breakfast, Ray and Benjie headed for the feed room. Skipper came bounding behind them. He loved to be wherever the boys were. After him came Engine, the lazy black cat that had scared Aunt Mandy when he was a kitten. Benjie turned back to look at Engine.

"Remember the time I put Engine on Aunt Mandy's lap when she was sleeping, and when she woke up and thought it was a rat?" he asked, grinning sheepishly.

"Of course I do," Ray chuckled. He looked back at Engine too. "I wonder if Aunt Mandy would remember."

They knew Aunt Mandy was getting more and more forgetful. She was stiff and lame. But she did not want to use a cane to walk, and she did not want to be in a wheelchair either. Benjie knew he would love to push her around in one. He hoped someday she would come to visit again. Surely she would enjoy a fast wheelchair ride.

"I think Shep would rather take a nap than follow us around," Ray was saying. Shep had started to come, but then he changed his mind and lay down under the hedge. "He is sure to come if he hears Skipper barking."

Ray stopped to get the shovel and some buckets. Now they were all set.

The feed room was a mess. Some mice had built their nests under the feed sacks. The sparrows had moved in too, and made great bulging nests in the rafters. They thought the feed room was just the place to take up nesting and raise their babies. Long feed sack strings hung haphazardly from their nests.

"Sparrows make their nests in such a haphazard way," Ray remarked.

Benjie looked at Ray. "What does that mean?" he asked.

"Haphazard?" Ray stopped for a moment to

think. "Why, it means like they make their nests kind of by chance. Whatever is around, they use. Take a robin. His nest is made just right, with mud and fine grass and stuff. But sparrows' nests are more untidy looking. Look at all the strings hanging from them, and feathers and what not."

"They just use whatever they find," Benjie agreed, "and parts of their nesting stuff hangs down. Here is some on the floor."

They did not want sparrows in the feed room! So they set to work with a will. Benjie climbed up and pulled down the nests. Ray worked at cleaning up the mess on the floor. They were both glad that by this time all the baby sparrows had learned to fly. The nests were empty. Even though the boys did not like English sparrows, they did not want them to suffer.

Skipper pranced around Ray as he worked, and did his best to get in the way. He sniffed around the feed sacks. He jumped up to snap at the empty nests as Benjie tossed them down from the rafters. When he caught the scent of sparrows in them, he began yapping excitedly and tearing around in circles. Shep awoke from his nap and, just as Ray had expected, came nosing to the doorway.

Soon there was a confused state of things. Benjie's hat had fallen off, and he had bits of nesting material in his hair. Over his head hung a long white string with several brown feathers. Ray was moving sacks of feed and every few

99

minutes shouting, "There goes a mouse!" Cats were underfoot chasing the mice, while the dogs barked wildly and chased each other.

In the house, Ellen helped Mom as much as she could. When the dishes were done, and the kitchen was in order, Ellen looked pleadingly at Mom. "Please, could I go help clean the feed room? Please, Mom! It's always so exciting."

Mom looked doubtfully at her daughter. "You'll get so dusty and dirty, Ellen," she began. Then she looked at Ellen's downcast face and remembered how she used to enjoy helping her brothers clean out the corncrib, or the feed room when she was a little girl. No matter how dirty she became, it was much more interesting than staying in the house.

Mom looked around the kitchen. "You did your work well, Ellen. You can go for a while. I used to enjoy helping my brothers too."

Ellen's face lit up. "Did Aunt Ruth like to help too?"

"Yes, she did," and Mom smiled, remembering. "One time she fell into the watering trough while she was watching the horses drink. She was standing on the edge of the trough so she could see better."

"How old was she?" Ellen tried to imagine Aunt Ruth, Alta and Nathan's mother, so little that she could fall into a watering trough.

"Hmmm . . . maybe six or seven. Mom scolded

us both. We were not to stand on the trough, and it's a wonder the horses didn't bite one of us."

While Mom talked, she tied a scarf over Ellen's head so her hair would not get so dusty. Then she sent her to put on an old dress that was so faded you couldn't tell what color it had been.

When Ellen returned in the old dress, Mom nodded approvingly. "Now be careful and try not to get too dirty," she said.

"Oh, thank you, Mom!" Ellen said, as she skipped happily out the door. Before Ellen even got close to the feed room, she heard barks and shouts. She hurried because she didn't want to miss anything. As she ran, she smiled to herself. She had learned a new word from Alta. Now she could use it.

"What a *din!*" she exclaimed as soon as she saw Ray. Ray looked surprised. He was moving a sack and his face was very dusty.

"I know what it means," Ellen said eagerly. "It means an uproar or a lot of noise. I heard you way off."

"Well, it is no wonder. With all these cats, and two dogs, and Benjie shouting every time he sees a mouse nest."

When Dad stopped in to see how the children were getting along, they were almost finished. The cement floor was swept. The sacks were stacked neatly. The buckets were in order. Dad looked around approvingly.

"You did a good job," Dad praised them. He looked up at the rafters. "It is high time we get this closed right so the sparrows can't get in. They make such a mess on the floor and over the feed sacks. Maybe I can get that done this afternoon, with you boys to help me. Did you see any sign of rats?" Dad knew how much damage rats could do.

"No," Benjie said, "but we found mice."

"Well, I'm glad if you didn't see any rats. I've seen Shep with one sometimes. With him and Skipper and the cats around, we shouldn't have too much rat trouble."

After supper that evening, Ray got out the encyclopedia with R words. "Here it says rats are the most serious animal threat to man," he announced.

Ellen's eyes were wide. "You mean a rat could hurt Dad?" she asked.

Ray looked at Ellen. He enjoyed explaining things to his brothers and sisters.

"Rats carry the germs of diseases," he said. "And they kill poultry and baby lambs and pigs. They would even bite a baby in a crib if they had a chance."

Ellen looked horrified. "Oh, we must never leave Ruth alone in her crib!" she gasped.

Mom's nose wrinkled with distaste. She hated rats, and she did not even like to talk about them. "You are scaring the children, Ray," she said.

"Listen," Dad spoke up. "I have read that such things happen, if a place is infested with rats. But we do not have rats in the house. Even if there were one in the basement, it would be very unlikely to come upstairs, much less be bold enough to bite a person. That usually happens only when rats are very hungry and houses are rundown and dirty, or if there are many rats together, as in some slums of the cities."

Ray was still poring over the encyclopedia. "It says there are about 120 kinds of rats, but the best known ones are black rats and brown rats. Most of the other kinds live in areas uninhabited by man."

Benjie remembered what uninhabited meant. Maybe chiggers and rats had something in common.

"We inhabit this house, so no rats can live here!" Benjie announced. Then he stopped and thought about that. Suppose he had to live in the slums and would see rats running about in the street, or maybe even in the house!

"There is something worse than rats," Dad said quietly. He was holding Toby, who was nearly asleep. "Can anyone guess what it is?"

"Is it spiders?" Ellen asked. Ellen did not like spiders.

"No, Ellen. It is sin. Rats are a threat to our bodies, but sin is a threat to our souls. Allowing sin to control one's life is far worse than letting rats take over our house! When a person sins he needs to take it to God right away and ask His forgiveness, so that sin does not grow in his heart and produce more sin."

"I'm glad we don't have rats," Benjie said soberly. "I am glad, too, that I can be sorry when I do something I shouldn't."

"So am I," Ray said, closing the encyclopedia. "That is what the minster preached about on Sunday, wasn't it? We have the privilege of repenting and doing right, instead of being stoned as they were in the Old Testament, before Jesus came."

Chapter 12

Getting Acquainted
With Danny

"Well, well." Uncle Albert pulled at his long beard. His eyes twinkled. "So you boys think you want another boy around?"

"Of course we do!" Benjie almost shouted.

Uncle Alberts and Danny had arrived the evening before. Ray and Benjie had been ready and waiting for them, and Benjie knew right away that Danny would be another friend for him.

Danny did not look like Benjie had expected. Danny was short. His legs and arms were short. Even his hands were short! Ray was taller than Danny, even though Danny was thirty-five years old. Danny could run, but not fast.

The first thing Danny did when he got out of

the car was give everyone a hug. "You're a shorty," he told Benjie and they all had to laugh.

When the men and boys set out for a walk around the farm, Danny did not want to walk beside Uncle Albert. Oh my, no! He wanted to walk with Dad. Uncle Albert just smiled. Later, when Danny wandered off to say hello to Engine, Uncle Albert explained.

"That is the way Danny is," he said. "He never meets a stranger, because everyone is his friend. It would be nice if all of us had his friendly nature. But the funny thing is, when he is here now, he doesn't want to have much to do with me. And if he is here with you and you get company, or go somewhere, he will act as though he likes the other people better."

Uncle Albert chuckled. "He has a lot of notions, and he loves to imagine and pretend. He will spend the whole morning playing church. He will be the preacher and preach to his imaginary congregation."

Ray and Benjie listened closely. It would be very different, having a friend like Danny.

"You need to be firm with him," Uncle Albert advised. "He has not been very healthy. And when a child is sick and has special problems it is not easy to know what to do. It was easier for his parents to let him have his own way."

"I understand," Dad said. "We want to do our best for him."

"He can be easily upset," Uncle Albert continued, "but he is just as quick to forget it. It's amazing how fast he learns and picks up things, the bad as well as the good. Although his mind is innocent, we have to protect him carefully from bad attitudes and ideas. Danny needs training and teaching, just as normal children do."

Soberly Dad stroked his beard. "All a man can take to heaven is his children, and even then it is not truly in our power to do so. But it is such a responsibility—teaching and training our children."

Ray and Benjie listened quietly. Then they heard Danny's cheerful voice behind them. He had grown tired of Engine and was now talking to Shep.

Shep wagged his tail slowly, as if he were not sure what to think of Danny. But Danny patted him on the head and kept on saying, "Nice dog. Nice dog." Shep relaxed. He loved attention.

Benjie watched Danny closely. He had worried about how Danny would treat Shep, but now he could see that Danny loved Shep too.

When Uncle Alberts left the next afternoon, Danny did not mind. Already he had accepted this new family as his own.

The following morning, Dad had a little talk with the boys as they did the chores together. "Never tease Danny," Dad cautioned them. "He cannot reason and think in the same way you do."

"But he is smart in other ways, isn't he?" Ray asked.

"Yes, he is. He can remember the names of almost everybody he meets."

"And he remembers their birthdays," Ray said.

"He even knows when Aunt Mandy's birthday is," Benjie added. "And as soon as he got here, he pretended to be Aunt Mandy. He said she walks like this." Benjie tried to imitate how Danny had walked.

Dad and Ray had to laugh. "Well, Danny will likely do some funny things," Dad said. "He likes to make you laugh. So laugh with him. But not *at* him. Never make fun of him."

Benjie thought about what Dad was saying. *Laugh with Danny, but not at him.* "How will Danny know we are not laughing *at him?*" Benjie wondered.

Dad pulled at his beard and thought for a little. "For instance, suppose you were walking into the schoolhouse and you dropped your lunch pail. Everything would roll out on the floor. The containers would break open and slop food on the desks and the floor and your clothes. Instead of helping you pick up your lunch, the children would point at you and laugh. They'd say, 'Look at Benjie! What a clumsy boy!' and laugh some more. How would you feel?"

"I would feel so ashamed," Benjie answered quickly. "I hope it never happens."

Dad went on. "But if you were telling your friends a funny story, or imitating something you knew was humorous, you would not mind if your friends laughed. Like just now when you imitated Danny walking like Aunt Mandy. You knew it would be funny, and we all had to laugh together. That was laughing *with* you."

"Yes," said Benjie, "that laughing did not make me feel embarrassed."

"You could tell the difference," Dad said, "and Danny will be able to tell the difference as well. When Danny is having fun too, that is laughing *with* him. If Danny is feeling ashamed, that is laughing *at* him. It comes under the word respect. Always respect the feelings of others. If we truly love people, we will treat them with respect."

"Respect," Benjie repeated slowly, as if feeling the word out.

"It means being polite and kind, doesn't it?" Ray said.

"Yes," Dad agreed, "treating others with esteem; regarding them more highly than one's self; following the Golden Rule—that is so important, so necessary."

"It's the best rule, isn't it?" Benjie said. He thought of Aunt Mandy. "If Aunt Mandy comes again, I want to treat her with respect too."

"Indeed, yes," Dad encouraged. "Everyone we meet, we want to treat with respect. No matter how old or young they are, or how they look, or how different they may be. Sometimes we see someone who looks or acts odd, but that never gives us a reason to be less than respectful."

"Al Camp was odd, wasn't he?" Benjie said.

"Well, he was different," Dad replied kindly. "That is what makes life interesting. If everyone were the same, think of how dull it would be."

"Suppose everyone were me," Benjie said, trying to imagine how that would be. "Or suppose everyone were Ray, or Dad."

Benjie shook his head. "I'm glad God made everything just as He did," he said.

"So am I." Dad looked at his watch. "It's time for breakfast. Let's go right away."

At the table, Danny sat beside Ray, with Benjie on the other side. Danny was pleased. Ray and Benjie were his friends. When Dad read the morning chapter, Danny wanted a Bible too. He pretended to read even though he couldn't.

When Dad and the boys went out to finish the chores, Danny stayed inside. Returning to the house later, Benjie found Danny playing church. Danny was preaching to imaginary people. Benjie sat down on a chair to listen. Danny smiled, pleased. Now he preached louder than ever. He waved his arms, then cleared his throat. With a grand flourish, he picked up the glass of water that Ellen had set on a chair in front of him. In church, the minister had a glass of water in front of him in case his throat became dry. And it would have been unheard of, for Danny to preach without a glass of water!

Then Ray called Benjie to come outside. This time Danny wanted to go along out. Danny could not walk as fast as Benjie. *Now I will treat Danny with respect,* Benjie thought to himself. He walked slower too, instead of hurrying on ahead.

"There is a late sparrow's nest in this pine tree," Ray said, as they approached him. "We should get rid of it so we don't have anymore sparrows around this place. I'm too big to climb up, but you can, Benjie."

Nimbly Benjie climbed up, from one branch to the other, until he got to the nest.

The father sparrow scolded, and the mother sparrow scolded. All the work they had put into that untidy nest and now it was being torn down! Shep and Skipper heard the angry birds and came running, barking excitedly. Then Ellen hurried outside to see what was going on.

"There are eggs in this nest," Benjie announced. He reached into the nest and threw an egg down to the ground.

Benjie was so intent on the nest that he did not notice Ellen approaching. He reached in for the rest of the eggs and threw them down as hard as he could.

There was a little scream from Ellen. Benjie stared, open-mouthed, down at his sister. He had thrown the eggs right on Ellen's head! Now she was half crying as she hurried into the house. One egg had burst and was plastered into her hair.

Ellen did not cry easily, but a smelly broken sparrow egg in her hair was too much.

Benjie quickly climbed down the tree and ran toward the house. Ray had been gathering up the untidy nesting material from the grass. He knew Mom did not want that lying in the yard, but now he followed Benjie, hurrying inside to find Ellen. Danny had watched all this, and now, he, too, trotted off toward the house as fast as his short legs would go.

"I'm sorry!" Benjie burst out as soon as he got inside. "Mom, I didn't know Ellen was under the tree!"

Mom was unbraiding Ellen's hair. She was going to wash Ellen's head as quickly as possible.

Mom turned to look at Benjie. "I know you did not do it on purpose," she said kindly. Mom felt as sorry for Benjie as she did for Ellen. "It will wash out," she comforted.

Ellen gave a few more sniffs. "It's all right, Benjie," she choked. "It just smells so bad!"

Danny stood in the doorway, his eyes big. "Is Ellen's head broke?" he asked. He came closer, then stopped and held his nose. "Whew! Ellen stinks. Egg stinks." He made a very queer face. "Come Benjie, let's go."

"Yes, go back and finish cleaning up the mess," Mom said. "Thankfully we have plenty of shampoo and water."

After Ellen's head was clean again, she could see the funny side of things. "I always want to watch out when Benjie is up in a tree," she said, laughing.

Danny could not forget what had happened. The next time he preached, his sermon was mostly about Benjie and the sparrow nest and the egg that fell on Ellen's head.

Ray and Benjie could hardly wait to take Danny to a real church service with them.

"When we get to church, you need to shake hands," Benjie told Danny, when Sunday morning finally came. Danny nodded. He knew that. He could hardly wait.

"And you have to sit quietly and listen to the sermon," Benjie added.

"No. Listen to the preacher," Danny corrected.

"He doesn't know what sermon means," Ray said.

Dad decided that Danny would sit with him instead of going with the other boys. He did not want Danny to make a disturbance, for Danny found it hard to sit still.

The church services were at Enos's folks'

place, so it did not take long to get there. Dad took Danny with him and went to greet the other men. Danny smiled and shook hands.

Enos's grandfather Mose was there. He had a cane and wore hearing aids. Danny did not put out his hand when he came to old Mose.

"Shake hands," Dad told him.

Danny shook his head, but Dad put his hand firmly on Danny's shoulder. Slowly, looking pouty, Danny shook hands with Mose.

Dad was puzzled. What had come over Danny? He was usually so friendly. Was it because Mose was old? Didn't Danny like old folks? Dad's brow had a little frown. If that was the case, he would have to do something about it.

In church, Mom could see Dad and Danny without turning her head. Dad, with his eyes on the minister, did not notice at first what Danny did. When someone coughed, Danny turned and glared at that person. A few minutes later, Danny coughed, too, and Mom knew he was pretending he had a cold.

When a little boy sitting next to Danny blew his nose, Danny looked at him and said "Sshh!" and held his finger to his lips. Then he pulled at his ear to show the boy that it hurt his ear to hear him. The little boy stared at Danny, fascinated.

Mom saw all this and felt as though she had to motion Dad to keep his eye on Danny. She could see that Dad was so interested in what the preacher was saying that he had forgotten all about Danny.

It was when Danny blew his own nose, loudly, that Dad turned and looked at him. Danny looked back at Dad. Quietly, Danny put his handkerchief in his pocket again. He smiled at the little boy beside him; then he looked at the preacher. He glanced back at Dad to see if Dad was still watching him. Since he was, Danny put on his best-behavior look. He sat up straight and watched the preacher.

After church was over, Danny went outside with Ray and Benjie.

"Who is your company?" Enos asked.

"It's Danny, our new friend," Benjie said. "He is staying with us for a while."

The boys crowded around Danny. Danny beamed. Without anyone telling him to, he shook hands with all of them.

When Sammy blew his nose, Danny frowned and said, "Too loud. Hurts my ears." The boys had to laugh.

Then Nathan stepped up to Ray. Turning to Danny, he said, "Ray is my cousin."

Danny looked at Nathan. "You my cousin too," he said, "and Benjie my cousin." Then he waved his hand. "All of you my cousins."

"Yes, we can all be cousins," one of the bigger boys said.

When it was time to go in for lunch, every boy wanted to sit beside Danny.

On the way home from church that afternoon, Mom told Dad how Danny had acted.

"I need to keep my eye on him," Dad said. "He does just what he feels like doing. He does not hide his feelings."

Dad thought for a bit. "I guess we could take a lesson from him. He does not hide his feelings, bad or good. We grown-ups can pretend to love our fellowman while inside we hide jealous or hateful feelings. But Danny is just like a child. He shows everything he feels. And that reminds me. Why didn't he like Mose?"

When they got home, the boys had already changed their clothes and were ready to do the chores. They had had a pleasant walk home with Danny.

"Now, Danny, why didn't you want to shake hands with Mose?" Dad asked. "Mose is a kind old man. We want to be friends with everyone."

Danny looked down. He frowned and shook his head.

"Why don't you like Mose?" Dad asked.

"I want hearing aids too," Danny sniffed.

"And that is why you did not want to shake his hand?" Dad glanced at Mom.

"I want a cane," Danny said. "My ears hurts and my legs hurts."

"I see." Dad's eyes twinkled but he managed

116

to keep a straight face. "Well, we have an old cane upstairs in the attic that you can use. And maybe we can check around and see if we can find some old hearing aids for you."

Danny looked up. His face brightened with a smile. "I love Mose," he said eagerly. "Mose my friend."

So that was it. By the time the boys began the afternoon chores, Danny was hobbling about on the cane that Ray had fetched for him.

Dad chuckled as he watched. Then he turned to Mom. "He was jealous of Mose," Dad said, "but the cane solved that problem."

Chapter 13

A Trip to Town

One morning after breakfast, Uncle Marks stopped in on their way to town.

"I wish you could go along," Nathan said to his cousins, as he hopped down from the back of the wagon.

"I wish so too," Ray said, leaning on his hoe. He and Benjie had been on their way to the garden.

"Where is Danny?" Nathan asked, looking around.

"He said it's too hot in the garden, so now he is playing church again," Ray said.

Dad had come in from the barn, and he and Uncle Mark were already deep in conversation. Aunt Ruth hurried off the wagon and toward the house.

"We can't stay long," Uncle Mark called after her.

"I know," Aunt Ruth called back. "We can't stay long," she repeated to Mom, who met her at the door and ushered her into the house, "but I know how it is when those two start talking. I'll stand here at the window so I can see when Mark is ready to go. Is there anything you need in town? And we would love to have your children go along."

A few minutes later Uncle Mark was picking up the lines. He looked toward the house. Aunt Ruth had noticed him preparing to leave and came bustling outside. Mom followed her. Ellen stood on the porch, and Danny was peering out the window.

"We'd be glad to have your children go with us," Uncle Mark said in an undertone to Dad.

Dad looked at the boys. They were so busy talking to Nathan that they had not heard a word. Dad looked up as Aunt Ruth and Mom approached.

"Well," Dad said, "I don't mind, if Anna doesn't."

Even without asking, Mom knew what Dad meant.

"What about Danny?" Uncle Mark asked. "We'd have room for him too." So it was decided.

Ray and Benjie were delighted. They hurried inside to get Danny. "And to think, we never even asked to go along!" Benjie marveled. "It's almost too good to be true!"

"Well, you know Dad and Mom like to give us good things," Ray replied.

"They are the best parents!" Benjie said. "But Uncle Marks are good too. Come on, Danny. Do you want to go along to town?" Benjie was getting his other hat—the one Aunt Mandy had given him. The hat was getting small for him, but that pleased Benjie. It showed that he was growing.

Danny lost no time in getting outside and into the wagon. The wagon had two seats. Danny settled himself on the seat behind Uncle Mark and Aunt Ruth. Ellen and Alta sat beside him. The other boys sat on the floor of the wagon, with their feet hanging over the back edge. Then they were off, bound for town.

Uncle Mark wanted to stop at the feed mill. He also had a shoe to leave at the cobbler's shop. Aunt Ruth needed to take Alta to the dentist, and she needed some groceries. When Ray and Benjie heard of all the stops they needed to make, they were even more pleased.

Ahead of them on the road, they saw Harvey and his brother Enos. They were driving a new horse. The horse was not used to this road. He wanted to look on both sides of the road. He shied at a stick. Then he lifted his head and gave a great loud neigh. The poor horse was bewildered. He did not know where he was. No doubt he was lonely for his old home and the horses there.

"Pass. Let's pass," Danny was saying. Danny loved to go fast.

When Danny's parents had to take him to the city doctor, Danny always wanted to sit in the front seat of the van. He would tell the driver to pass the truck or car or whatever was in front of them. If the driver did not pass the truck, Danny would look cross. If the driver did pass him, Danny would cheer. "Good driver!" he would say.

It was the same in the buggy. Danny wanted to pass anyone he saw. Now Uncle Mark's wagon was right behind Harvey's. Uncle Mark knew if he passed Harvey it might perk up the new horse. The horse would get his mind on Uncle Mark's horse and want to follow him. Maybe he would not feel so lonely.

Carefully Uncle Mark guided his horse out and past the other rig. Harvey and Enos waved and everyone waved back. All but Danny. He was so busy cheering and praising Uncle Mark.

"Good driver, good driver," he said over and over. "Not a slowpoke. Mark can go fast!"

When they were almost to town, they came up behind a pony and cart. Uncle Mark did not pass it, but Danny leaned forward eagerly.

"Pass, pass," he said.

"No, not this time," Uncle Mark replied, smiling down at Danny. Danny sat back in the seat. He slumped down. His face was as long as a face could be.

"Slowpoke. Slowpoke," he mumbled. But soon he forgot it. Danny never stayed upset long.

When they got to town, Uncle Mark dropped Aunt Ruth and the girls off at the dentist's office. Then he and the boys drove to the shoe cobbler's shop.

When they entered the shop, the cobbler was bent over, fixing a shoe, but he came hurrying over to meet them.

"Hello, hello," the cobbler said. He did not stop to hear if Uncle Mark said hello or not. He kept right on talking. "Yes, I know you. You are the man that left a shoe on the door step."

Ray and Benjie looked at each other and grinned. They had not forgotten that other time they came to town with Uncle Mark. Finding the cobbler's door locked, Uncle Mark had left his old shoe sitting on the steps outside the shop.

Uncle Mark showed the cobbler his old, worn shoe. The cobbler looked at it carefully. Just watching the way he looked at it, you could tell the cobbler loved shoes.

Carefully he felt the sole. "Hmmm, yes," he said, "I can fix it, good and tight. You'll get some more wear out of it yet." It was plain the cobbler loved his work, and he was all business.

As Danny walked around in the little shop, he pointed to this and that shoe. "Where other shoe? Just one foot?" he asked, puzzled.

Ray tried to explain to him that this was a

shoe-mending shop. Suddenly Danny thought of something. He had forgotten his cane! So far, since Sunday, he'd had a lame leg. He had not been able to walk without that cane.

Now again, Danny was lame and had a sore foot. He wanted to take off his shoe and leave it there for the cobbler to fix. Once the shoe was fixed, his foot would no longer be sore.

Ray realized it would have been better if he had not explained to Danny that these shoes needed fixing. The boys crowded around Danny and in hushed voices tried to explain to him that the cobbler was busy. He did not have time to fix a shoe then and there. If a shoe needed fixing, it would have to be left at the shop like all the other shoes.

But Danny shook his head unhappily. By now several other customers had entered the little shop. They eyed the boys. They could tell something was going on. Danny kept shaking his head.

"My foot hurts," he complained. He took a few steps and nearly sank to the floor to show how serious it was. "My shoe needs nail," he insisted.

Uncle Mark turned to see what was wrong. The cobbler was watching sharply, intently. "What's the trouble?" he asked. It was plain that he did not want a fuss in his place of business.

Ray turned apologetically toward the cobbler.

123

"He says his foot hurts," he began. Ray was going to explain that Danny was pretending, but the cobbler was no longer listening. He was looking sharply at Danny.

The cobbler's mouth twitched, and suddenly he had to cough. He rose from his stool. "Come here, young man," he motioned to Danny.

Eagerly Danny came. He forgot about limping, but he was pointing to his "sore foot."

"I'll attend to your shoe right away," the cobbler promised. "A sore foot—that is not good."

Danny's face brightened. He beamed at the cobbler. "My buddy, my friend," he said as he sat down on a little stool. Benjie helped him take off his shoe.

Then Danny handed the shoe to the cobbler. Never had the cobbler looked so serious or so business like. He studied the shoe carefully, while everyone looked on.

The cobbler was muttering to himself. "Hurts his foot, he says. Can't put this off for another day." He looked up at Danny, who was right at his elbow and watching every move he made. "I'll have this done in a jiffy, young man, if you don't mind waiting."

Why, Benjie thought to himself, *the cobbler is treating Danny with respect.* As for Danny, he looked as pleased as possible.

The cobbler reached for a nail. "Hmmm, no,

that is too big." He kept fumbling around in his drawer. "There, this is just right," he said. Then he pounded on the shoe. He felt it again. "Now, young man, let's see if this isn't better."

Danny sat down, and Benjie helped him put his shoe back on. Carefully Danny stood up. "It is fixed!" he announced triumphantly. Then he gave the cobbler a great hug. "My buddy, my friend!" he exclaimed.

Everyone was laughing. The other customers were watching, smiling, and nodding.

"What do I owe you?" Uncle Mark asked respectfully.

But the cobbler shook his head. He wiped his eyes with the back of his hand. No one had ever before hugged the cobbler for fixing his shoe, much less a shoe that didn't need fixing.

"Your time," Uncle Mark insisted. He knew the cobbler was a busy man. The cobbler kept shaking his head.

"I'll try to have your shoe fixed by the next time you come in," was all he would say. "And," he paused, "bring these fine young men along any time."

Now that his shoe was "fixed," Danny did not think about a lame leg. He walked briskly. He felt important. The cobbler had fixed his shoe. Wherever they went, Danny attracted people's friendly smiles.

Uncle Mark and Aunt Ruth finished all their

business in town. They made an extra stop, too, for Uncle Mark treated everyone to ice cream cones.

They arrived home at noon, just in time for dinner. And then, because Mom insisted, Uncle Marks stayed to eat with them. Mom had opened a jar of canned chicken. She mixed up dressing and baked that with the chicken. She made mashed potatoes and gravy. She served tasty green beans, that she had picked that morning, and sliced tomatoes and coleslaw.

"The cabbage needs to be used," Mom said, when Aunt Ruth fussed about such a big dinner. For dessert they ate fresh peaches and cream, and a warm apple crumb cake with whipped cream on top.

"Wouldn't Al Camp have enjoyed this dinner?" Nathan remarked at the table. It was surprising how hungry they all were, in spite of the ice cream they'd eaten.

Danny did not talk much during the meal. He was too busy eating. He did not notice that the grown-ups were talking about him.

"He called Mr. Harper, there at the feed mill, a 'fine big man' and gave him a hug," Uncle Mark said. "You know what a big man Mr. Harper is. And Danny said his worker was 'strong' because he helped carry out the sacks of feed. And another man was 'smart,' because he had a checkbook in his shirt pocket.

Uncle Mark paused to take a second helping of potatoes and gravy. "When we were ready to leave the feed mill," he went on, "Danny took it into his head that he wanted a sack of feed too. So the workers put a handful of this and that into a sack and said it was just the thing to feed to the calves."

"I hope he wasn't a bother," Dad said, though he had to smile at the stories.

Uncle Mark smiled too. "No, he made the trip pretty special," he said.

Aunt Ruth agreed. "But next time I hope I'll see more of him," she said. "He spent so much time with Mark, while we ladies did our separate errands. Maybe he and the boys could come over sometime."

Ray and Benjie smiled. Going to Uncle Marks was one of their favorite things to do!

After everyone had finished eating, the children went outside under the shade tree. The adults sat around the table inside to finish talking. Through the open windows they could hear Danny "preaching" to the other children.

Uncle Mark was not done talking about his day in town with Danny. "I could see that everyone who met Danny liked him. They took to him right away. He is so warm and friendly. You know, some people kind of turn you off. They act uppity, or as if they would rather not talk with you. No matter how good-looking a person is, if he does not have a warm, kind expression, you just want to shy away."

"That is right," Dad agreed. "People can build walls in their minds. They may be shy and lonely, but they are afraid if they reach out to other people, they may be rejected. So rather than getting hurt, they act aloof and indifferent." Dad leaned back in his chair.

"But with Danny it is different," he went on. "He shows exactly what he feels. He does not hide his feelings under a mask. I wish we could all be more like Danny in that respect. He is just himself."

"He has a mission on this earth same as each one of us has," Uncle Mark concluded. "I think of them as angels among us—these children who never grow old in their minds. They stay innocent all their lives."

Uncle Mark looked at the clock. "But we have to be going. Thanks for the delicious meal. And thanks for letting us take your children and Danny with us!"

"It meant a lot to the children too," Dad said. "Thank *you* for taking them."

Outside, and unnoticed by the children, Dad and Uncle Mark stopped to listen to Danny. Danny was preaching about the cobbler.

"The cobbler is good man. Fixed shoe. My buddy, the cobbler. But Benjie bad. He let egg plop on Ellen's head." And as he said that,

Danny motioned with his hands. One hand threw down the imaginary egg. The other hand was Ellen's head. "Plop," he repeated. Then he put his head down and pretended to cry.

"Well, children, it's time we go," Uncle Mark said. He was sorry to put a stop to the good time they were having.

Aunt Ruth was coming out the door. "Now I can go home, Anna, without thinking about having to make dinner. It's your turn to visit *us* now, and we'll be looking forward to that. Just let us know when it suits you."

Chapter 14

Goats in the Garden

Uncle Mark's family was in good spirits as they drove home from Uncle David's house that afternoon. Mark had picked up the feed he needed. His shoe was at the cobbler's to get fixed. He'd been able to find what he needed at the hardware store. Getting the little things done and off his mind was a good feeling.

Aunt Ruth was just as cheerful. She had taken Alta to the dentist. She had purchased the necessary groceries. She found thread on sale. Just what she needed for Mark's shirt. And they'd had a good dinner. Now she wouldn't have to hustle around to get a meal ready at home.

They had all enjoyed having Ray, Benjie, and

Ellen along, and having Danny go with them made it all the more special.

As they rode home they talked about Danny. "He has been here only one Sunday, but he already knows all the children and babies' names in church," Aunt Ruth marveled.

Then she explained what Danny had done on Sunday. Danny loved packages. When he saw several in the washhouse where the women and girls had put their wraps, Danny gathered up those packages and put them in Uncle David's buggy.

Then there was a grand mix-up because the owners could not find their bags. When Ellen went out to the buggy, she found them and took them back in. Of course, the ladies who brought them were relieved to know the packages were not lost.

"What was in the packages?" Nathan asked curiously.

"Well, not so much. But someone left a diaper at church the other time, so that was in one bag. And someone brought a book along that they thought Enos's mother might want to read since she isn't feeling well." Ruth turned around to look at Nathan and Alta. Alta was half asleep.

"Anyway," she finished, "Danny was not happy that those bags were not on the buggy when they went to go home. He insisted they were his bags."

131

Mark chuckled. "There are no dull moments with Danny around," he said. He clucked to the horse and slapped the reins against his broad back.

They all felt contented and relaxed. It had been such an interesting day. Aunt Ruth was sleepy. Little Neil was asleep on her lap. She glanced back and saw that Nathan was nodding too.

They had no idea what had been going on at home while they were gone. Amos, their sad-looking dog, came to meet them as they drove in the lane. He wagged and gave several purposeful barks. Usually Amos would be taking a nap when they came home.

"Maybe he was getting lonesome," Nathan suggested, as he awoke from his own little snooze.

Amos was a good, faithful dog. When Neil played in the sandbox, Amos stayed nearby. If something was out of the ordinary, he gave sharp little barks that told the family something was not right. When Uncle Mark was not at home, Amos was more watchful and looked more sad then ever. They all remembered the Sunday Mom was at home alone when Neil was a tiny baby. A car had driven in, and two men climbed out of the car and came to the house. Mom had never seen them before. But when Amos saw those men, he barked so fiercely that they hastily climbed into the car and drove away rapidly.

No one knew where Amos came from. He had first come around their house as a stray dog. Maybe someone had dropped him off. Perhaps he had wandered away from his original home. They had no idea why he looked so sad.

Now as they drove up to the house, they stared in surprise. Keturah, the goat, was in the garden! She looked at them placidly as they drove in. Her twin kids were in the yard, nibbling at Mom's rosebushes. The other two half-grown goats were in the garden with Keturah. They all looked innocently at the horse and wagon. Then they jumped into the air and frolicked around and tried to push each other down.

Wordlessly, Uncle Mark tied the horse to the fence. Aunt Ruth hurried inside with Neil and laid him in his crib. Silently, Nathan and Alta jumped off the wagon. What was there to say? The goats were out, and they all knew what that meant. It meant trouble. *Trouble spelled with a capital T,* Nathan thought to himself.

Aunt Ruth came back outside and looked grimly at the garden. Those goats had eaten the cabbage plants. They had eaten the strawberry plants. The rosebushes looked bare and sad, as they were stripped of all their leaves.

Keturah came and nudged Alta, while the kids

tried to play with Nathan. They had had a grand time feasting and romping in the garden, and now they were ready for some other excitement.

"I wish you'd take them all to the butcher!" Aunt Ruth said forcefully.

"Right now?" Uncle Mark asked. "I can't understand it. I thought the fence was as tight as a goat fence could be." Uncle Mark was feeling grim too. The goats had plenty to eat in the field they were in. There was a nice variety of weeds and grasses. Why weren't they content there?

"They didn't touch the potato plants," Aunt Ruth said, walking through the garden to check out the damage. "So apparently they don't like them. Why, when they already have more than they can eat, do they have to come into the garden?"

But no one could say—it is just the way goats are.

Nathan and his father put the goats back in their field. They found where the goats had pushed through the fence.

"I'm going back over to David's right away," Uncle Mark said, as he untied the horse. "David had some fencing left—all I'd need to fix the fence."

Everyone at the Mast's house was surprised when Uncle Mark drove in a short while later. Mom hurried outside. Maybe there had been an accident. Dad and the boys hurried out of the barn. They all stood around listening as Uncle Mark told them about the goats.

"Bad, bad goats!" Danny kept saying, over and over. The next time he played church, his sermon was about the bad goats, *and* his good buddy the cobbler, and Benjie, who let the egg plop on Ellen's head.

In the meantime, they all felt as sorry as could be for Uncle Marks.

"All those strawberry plants," Mom mourned.

"I know," Uncle Mark said. "But likely they will grow out again." Already Uncle Mark was feeling better.

"I've heard that to keep goats in, you need to put up a fence that would hold water," Dad said.

"In that case I'll need to put up a wall," Uncle Mark said, smiling.

Then they all turned as a horse and rider came galloping in the lane. It was Harvey. He reined in his horse, and it slowed to a stop reluctantly.

"This week's sign language class is scheduled for tomorrow evening instead of Friday night, as the teacher is planning on being gone Friday," Harvey announced. "This saves me another stop since you are here too," he said to Uncle Mark. Then after a few more words, he left.

"Well, I have to move on," Uncle Mark said. "I guess we will see you all tomorrow evening then."

Dad helped load the fencing. As Uncle Mark

left, he grinned and said, "By the way, any chance you'd be interested in buying some of our goats?"

"I'd have to ask Anna about that," Dad said, chuckling. "And I'm pretty sure I know what her answer would be."

Chapter 15

Sign Language Class

The next evening, the family scurried around getting ready to go to sign language class.

"Do you think Danny will be able to learn any signs?" Benjie asked. In the bustle and excitement, no one heard his question but Benjie really didn't care. He was talking to himself as much as to anyone else. He would just have to wait and see.

Benjie was enjoying the classes. All the dreading he had done had been so needless.

"It's just like they say," Ray told him. "Don't cross your bridge before you get there." Benjie knew what that meant. There was no use worrying about something. In his case, the dreaded bridge had been the sign language class.

To think of the hours a person spends

dreading and fretting about things! Instead, we should ask God for His help in whatever we dread and then leave the worry in God's hands. He will take care of it. Birds don't worry from one day to the next. They are not fretting and wondering where they will find their next day's breakfast.

It was really too bad, Benjie discovered, to fill up one's hours with needless worry, when those same hours could be filled with joy and thankful hearts and praising God for His help.

In the class that evening, Benjie learned the last few letters of the finger alphabet. Now he could sign the entire alphabet, from A to Z. Danny pretended he knew the signs too. He made all kinds of signs, and Ray and Benjie pretended to understand what he meant. Everyone enjoyed the class, including Danny. The more signs and motions, the better Danny liked it!

After the meeting a circle of boys gathered outside. Danny left Dad and walked over to join them.

Two visiting boys, Nelson and Leroy, stood there talking with the other boys. They had not noticed Danny before. Now, seeing him for the first time, they stared at him.

"Hey, he isn't bright," Nelson said.

"And he looks funny," Leroy added.

Then they laughed as if they had said something smart.

Benjie could not believe his ears. Ray and Nathan looked at each other. The visiting boys were making fun of Danny!

"You mean you guys put up with him?" Nelson was saying.

Ray took a deep breath. He would tell these boys a thing or two. But before he got a word out, Benjie spoke up.

"Maybe he isn't bright like you are," he said, "but in some ways he is smarter. And he knows better than to make fun of folks. He is just the way God made him."

"Is that so?" Nelson laughed. He looked around expecting the other boys to side with him. He had become acquainted with some of them the day before. "You are a regular rooster," he told Benjie scornfully.

Danny had not yet noticed the new boys. He was busy talking to another boy named Joel. Joel could not understand what all Danny was saying, but it surely was interesting. He thought Danny was very special.

"Egg went plop! Goats ate all the strawberries," Danny said excitedly. He motioned with his hands how the goats had jumped out of their pen.

"Am I your friend?" Joel asked.

"Joel my buddy. Joel my friend," Danny said. Danny could remember each boy's name. "Joel my friend," he repeated. Then Danny noticed

Nelson. He walked over and stopped in front of him. "What your name?"

Nelson was surprised. Before he thought (for ordinarily he would not have talked to someone like Danny), he answered, "My name is Nelson."

"Nelson my friend, my buddy," Danny said. He was bubbling with friendliness and goodwill. He loved this, being with the boys. In the darkness, he could barely make out who they were, but that did not matter.

Before anyone could say anything, Danny gave Nelson a hug. Nelson backed away. He looked taken aback.

Then a boy named Sammy stepped up. "Hey, Danny, am I your friend?" he asked.

"My buddy," Danny beamed. "Sammy my friend."

Sammy grinned.

"What about me?" Rob asked.

"Rob my buddy. One, two buddies. Sammy and Rob." Danny was fairly bursting with importance.

"What about me?" Enos asked.

"And me?" Another boy spoke up.

Danny spread out his arms. "Everyone my friend. Everyone my buddy," he chortled happily.

The boys had forgotten about Nelson and Leroy. In the dark, Danny never noticed Leroy at all. Nathan was asking Danny to tell them about the cobbler fixing his shoe. Now Danny tried to stand as tall as possible. He cleared his throat with the greatest importance. The boys crowded around.

Danny looked around the circle of faces. His manner was dignified. "Benjie," he said, motioning with his hand, "be quiet." How he loved this, having an audience!

He limped about to show the boys how his foot had hurt. Then he explained with many motions how the cobbler had fixed his shoe. And then he talked about the goats who ate the cabbages.

By now the parents were coming out of the schoolhouse. "Time to go," someone called. Several adults stopped to chat with Danny as they went to hitch up their horses.

Nelson and Leroy slunk away to their buggy. The evening had not turned out right. Instead of looking up to them, as some of the boys did at home, these boys had ignored them.

Nelson knew his younger brother, Leroy, would hardly have said anything to make fun of Danny if he hadn't. He knew it was wrong to make fun of others. But he made excuses to himself. *I wasn't actually making fun,* he thought. *And what does it matter? That boy, Danny, does not know the difference.*

But Nelson had a hollow feeling inside. He had wanted the boys to think he was smart and tough. But he had failed. What if he were in Danny's shoes? What if others treated him as he had treated Danny?

And deep down inside, strange as it was, he wanted to be Danny's friend.

Chapter 16

Danny Is Sorry

"I wonder what happened to my knife," Ray said a few days later. He looked at the circle of faces around the lunch table. "Has anyone seen it? I can't find it anywhere."

"You can't find your knife?" Dad repeated. He, too, looked around the table. *Was that a guilty look on Danny's face?* "Maybe you left it lying outside when you were making your box trap," he suggested.

Ray and Nathan had gotten the idea to each make a box trap. Then they would trap rabbits. They wanted to surprise Benjie by making him a trap too.

But Benjie didn't know that, and he was feeling like a left-out boy. Yesterday Nathan had come over with a message from Uncle Mark. Right away he and Ray had started talking about a certain book Nathan had brought along, but Benjie was not interested. He had taken Danny down to the creek, where they had a good time wading in the cool water.

The book had a lot of wood projects in it, and one of them was a box trap. Benjie knew if he had stayed at home the boys would have shared their plans with him. But it was easier to think it was Ray and Nathan's fault that he was not included.

By now the dinner conversation had moved on to other things.

"Right after dinner," Dad was saying, "I want you boys to take this pig medicine over to Uncle Mark. Be careful on the road with Pepper."

Suddenly Benjie began to feel better. "May Danny go too?" he asked. Surprisingly enough, Danny did not want to go. Dad looked at Danny again. Maybe he was just tired and needed a nap.

Pepper did not like to go away, much less after dinner! If ponies could grumble, Pepper would have. He tossed his head crossly and pranced around. Instead of backing nicely into the wagon shafts, he twisted and turned and pranced about. But Ray and Benjie were even more determined than the pony. Soon he was hitched up, and they were ready to go.

"Now come on, Pepper. Get going," Ray urged. He slapped Pepper with the reins. Pepper turned his head and looked back.

"He looks as cross as can be," Benjie said.

"And he is going to poke all the way."

But once they were on the road, Pepper lowered his head and trotted so briskly that they were surprised.

When they arrived at Uncle Mark's house, they were just in time to see Uncle Mark and Nathan bending over a bush in the yard. At first they did not know what was going on.

Uncle Mark had put a little fence around that bush. Just in case a goat got out, he wanted to be on the safe side. It was a special kind of shrub, and Aunt Ruth did not want anything to happen to it.

While Uncle Mark's family was eating dinner a few minutes earlier, they heard what they first thought was a child crying. When they went to look, they found that the littlest goat had somehow managed to get out of his field and inside the little fence around the shrub. It could not get out and it could not do anything that it wanted to do. So it bleated, and it sounded like a baby crying.

Uncle Mark looked disgruntled as he rescued the little kid. He was tired of goat trouble, but he tried to be patient. The goats on the other side of the fence seemed concerned about the little kid's bleating. As soon as Uncle Mark lifted the kid over his own fence, the other goats crowded around it.

"They act like the little goat is a hero," Nathan

said. "But I think Keturah should be giving it a scolding."

"I suppose goat mothers don't know any better," Uncle Mark said. He turned to his nephews. "Thank you for bringing this medicine over. Our neighbors want to use some of it, too. Now, won't you come in a while, or do you need to go back right away?"

"We can get a drink," Benjie stated. Then they had to laugh. When Dad gave the boys permission to get a drink at Uncle Marks, he knew it might take fifteen minutes.

Inside, Aunt Ruth and Alta were just finishing up the dishes. Aunt Ruth set a platter of cookies on the table to go with their drink. But instead of a drink of water, she had made lemonade. The boys talked as fast as they could while they ate.

Then it was time to go. They thanked Aunt Ruth for the snack and hurried out. Dad had work for them to do at home.

Pepper was pawing the ground eagerly. "He acts as though he has had to wait for hours," Benjie said. "He doesn't have any patience."

"Look at Keturah," Ray said. He stood looking at the goats. Keturah was standing on her hind legs trying to reach up into the cherry tree.

"If they hear us talking," Nathan told his cousins, "they will bleat as if they want to have their say too."

146

"It is never dull with goats around, is it?" Ray said.

"No indeed." Nathan was holding Pepper while the boys jumped into the cart, and then they were off. Pepper started off at a gallop. Benjie held his hat with one hand and clutched the side of the cart with the other. At the rate Pepper was going, he had to watch that he didn't fly off the cart.

No one was around when they passed Harvey and Enos's home. Their dog barked a time or two and then settled down for his nap.

At home, Mom and Ellen were folding the laundry. Then Mom carried the boys' clean clothes upstairs to put them away. She went to Danny's room first. Danny kept his room in nice order. Mom put his freshly washed clothes in a drawer. Then she looked again. There, under a handkerchief, was Ray's missing knife! Quickly Mom picked up the knife. Then she went out to find Dad, and showed him what she had found in Danny's drawer.

"I wondered if he might have gotten it," Dad said soberly. He was remembering Danny's guilty expression at the table. "He doesn't realize the seriousness of stealing, even though he knows he shouldn't do it. When he sees something he wants, he likely will take it."

"What should we do?" Mom wondered.

"Where is he?" Dad asked.

"He and Ellen are playing church under the shade tree," Mom answered. Dad and Mom went to find Danny.

"Now, Danny," Dad began, "This is Ray's knife, and Mom found it in your drawer."

Danny's face fell. "But I want a knife too," he said sadly.

"But you must not take what does not belong to you. That is wrong," Dad said.

Danny looked down.

"Hundred times sorry." He looked more sorry and woebegone than Dad and Mom had ever seen him.

When Ray and Benjie came home, they were surprised to see Dad, Mom, Ellen, and Danny in a circle under the shade tree. Toby and Ruth were taking their afternoon naps.

"Hundred times sorry," Danny told Ray as soon as he saw him. Ray looked puzzled.

"Danny had your knife up in his drawer," Dad explained, "and he wants to apologize."

"I'll let you use it sometimes," Ray offered. But he knew Danny should not have a knife to keep. It would be too easy for him to cut himself.

That evening Danny was not happy. "Ray stole my knife. Now I have no knife. Poor Danny," he muttered, shaking his head sadly. "Poor Danny. No knife."

They tried to explain that it was Ray's knife, but Danny could not understand.

"Come, Danny, let's play you are an auctioneer," Ray said. "You can sell the cows and we will buy them."

Danny brightened up. He loved being an auctioneer.

Ellen brought him his cardboard pipe to talk into like a microphone, and he was off. "Zero, forty, forty-five, forty-five, thirty, black cow sold to Ray who took my knife." Danny waved his arms. He gave a mighty cough and started in again.

"Forty, twenty, forty-five, forty-five, fifty, mean cow sold to Benjie who let the egg plop on Ellen's head."

The children cheered and laughed, and Danny was so wound up that he sold all the cows. Then, clapping his hands, he announced that the sale was over.

"And now it is bedtime," Mom said. She had enjoyed the sale too.

After Danny and the younger children were in bed, Dad talked to the boys. "You know that Danny cannot reason like you do," Dad said slowly. He wanted the children to understand how different it was for Danny. "His brain did not develop like yours did. Always be thankful that you have a sound mind. But remember that God has a purpose and plan for Danny, just as He has for everyone else.

"If you do wrong, you know better," Dad

continued, "but Danny may not, and he will imitate you. For instance, if you say bad words, Danny will do the same. Can you see the harm you would be doing?"

Soberly Ray and Benjie nodded. "He picks up the bad things as well as the good, doesn't he?" Ray pondered. Then Ray remembered what had happened in sign language class, when Nelson and Leroy made fun of Danny. He had forgotten all about it, but now he told Dad how the visiting boys had acted.

Dad looked serious. "Thank you, boys, for not joining in with them and laughing at Danny. I hope Nelson and Leroy will learn as they grow up that children like Danny are just as precious to God as everyone else is. Danny has feelings too. He feels it if someone is unkind to him. He feels it if someone makes fun of him. And when we do good or bad to other people, it is like we are doing it to Jesus."

"We should be kind to everyone," Mom said. "No matter who a person is."

"Yes, indeed," Dad agreed. "I do not want you boys to look down on Danny because he has a childlike mind."

"Oh, no. We don't want to," Benjie said quickly. "Even if he can't think like we do, he is still my friend."

"And it is going to be awfully dull when he goes home," Ray added. He stopped to think. "I wish we could give him something he would really like, to take with him when he leaves."

"Maybe some animals," Benjie suggested. Then they had to laugh. Danny liked to have paper animals. But if they did not look right to him, he took the scissors and cut their heads or tails off. So Danny had a number of headless animals.

"Enos said he wishes we'd let Danny come over to his house for several days," Benjie said.

"What did you tell him, Benjie?"

"I said it's best if he stays at one place."

"Yes, that is right," Dad agreed. "I'm glad you remembered that to tell him. We don't want to be selfish with Danny, but Danny is like a little boy. He needs someone to look after him like a parent."

The next morning Dad called Danny to him. "Let me have your hand, Danny," he said.

Pleased and smiling, Danny held out his hand.

"Now, come here, children," Dad went on. "I want you to look at Danny's hand. God made it in a very special way."

Ray, Benjie, and Ellen looked at Danny's open hand. Dad traced the lines in Danny's palm. "Notice this first line? Now look at your own."

Thoughtfully, they opened their own hands and studied them.

"Benjie, how is the first line in your palm different from Danny's?"

Benjie looked at his palm, then again at

Danny's. "Why, mine curves a little, but Danny's goes straight across," Benjie said, wonderingly.

"It is because he has an extra . . ." Ray hesitated. "What is it called?"

"Danny has an extra chromosome in the cells of his body," Dad explained.

Danny beamed. He looked down at his hand. Then he examined Ray's and Benjie's and Ellen's hands. Then he inspected Dad's and Mom's and Toby's hands. "Toby has shortie hand," he said, laughing.

Then Danny looked at his own open hand again.

"Do you see it, Danny?" Dad asked. "Your line goes straight across your palm."

Danny nodded. He felt very important with Dad looking at his hand. In fact, they were all studying Danny's hand. His hand was so plump. What cute, short hands Danny had. His fingers were short and stubby. But then, Danny was short all over. They loved Danny more than ever, because he was Danny! His shortness, and his plumpness, and his Oriental-looking features—everything about him—made Danny special. Yet it was the lovable boy Danny was inside that made him truly Danny.

* * * * *

The next day there was a letter from Uncle Alberts. They would be coming next week for a visit. If Aunt Mandy was able, she would come too. Then after their visit, Danny would go home with Uncle Alberts.

Now the whole household was in a fine state of nerves. Aunt Mandy was coming! One minute Benjie felt he would burst with excitement, and the next minute he felt terribly sad. He did not want Danny to leave. What would they do without Danny?

"That is the way life is," Ray said. "Changes come; some are good, and some are sad."

* * * * *

Benjie had forgotten the box traps. But the next morning Ray set one at Benjie's place at the table. "It's for you," Ray said, smiling with the pure joy of giving. "Nathan and I wanted to surprise you."

At first, Benjie did not know what to say. He remembered how he had felt, unhappy and left out. Now they had made him a trap of his own!

After breakfast they took it outside. Benjie dug a big carrot from the garden, with Danny watching. Ray tried to explain it to Danny. "A rabbit might come and be caught in the trap. But the rabbit would not be hurt."

Danny nodded. He liked rabbits.

"Thank you, Ray!" Benjie said over and over. He set his trap at one end of the orchard, and Ray set his at the other end.

Chapter 17

Aunt Mandy

The Mast family were all together in the kitchen when Aunt Mandy and Uncle Alberts came. Everyone rushed outside to greet the guests. Aunt Mandy was already trying to get out and Uncle Albert was saying, "Now wait a minute. Let me help you. Here, take my arm."

Uncle Albert was actually taking hold of Aunt Mandy's arm. No one knew Aunt Mandy better than Uncle Albert did. Aunt Mandy had a mind of her own, and the older she got, the more she became Aunt Mandy! She did not feel that Uncle Albert needed to tell her what to do. She was older than Uncle Albert. And he wasn't her uncle. Neither was Albert's wife Katie her aunt, even though everyone called her Aunt Katie.

Finally, Aunt Mandy was out of the car. Already Uncle Albert was unloading the wheel-chair from the trunk of the car. "Just wait, and you can sit down," he encouraged her.

Aunt Mandy frowned. "I do not need that thing."

"Here is your cane," Aunt Katie said, trying to be helpful. She knew Aunt Mandy did not like her cane or her wheelchair. But Aunt Mandy did not realize how tottery she was. Uncle Alberts did not want her to fall. It would be so easy for Aunt Mandy to break her hip.

By now, Dad and Mom were there—Mom on one side of Aunt Mandy and Dad on the other. Uncle Albert and Aunt Katie looked relieved.

"Now where is my box? My false teeth box?" Aunt Mandy was asking.

"Here. Here it is." Quickly Aunt Katie pressed it into Aunt Mandy's hand.

"Oh Aunt Mandy! I am so glad to see you!" Benjie exclaimed. "See? I am wearing the hat you gave me."

Aunt Mandy turned and looked sharply at Benjie. "And who is this young man?"

"Why, I am Benjie. Don't you remember me?" Then Benjie saw the false teeth box in Aunt Mandy's hand. He had made that box for Aunt Mandy when they had gone to visit her two years ago.

"I made that box for you, remember? When we visited you?" he asked anxiously.

155

Aunt Mandy frowned thoughtfully. "You made this for me?"

Aunt Mandy looked at the false teeth box. Then she looked at Benjie again. It seemed she was having a faint, faraway memory of Benjie.

Aunt Mandy loved children, but over the years her mind had been failing. She was getting more and more forgetful. Suddenly she smiled. "So you are Benjie, and you made me this box. Thank you, Benjie."

Ray stepped forward. "I am Ray. Benjie is my brother."

Aunt Mandy nodded. Even if she could not remember who these children were, she could still nod and smile kindly at them, and that was what she was doing. They helped Aunt Mandy into the house, and everyone else followed them in.

Aunt Katie took a deep breath. "I am certainly glad we are here."

"So am I," Mom said. "The trip must have been a strain."

"It was. But I am so glad we could bring Aunt Mandy. She enjoys a change, and even if she doesn't remember you, it does her good to be here. Now and then she remembers. Aunt Mandy has always been a special person."

"The children could hardly wait until you all came," Mom said, smiling. "And I was quite excited myself."

Meanwhile, Ellen and Danny were telling

Aunt Mandy their names. When Danny saw Aunt Mandy's cane, he promptly remembered that he had a lame leg too. He screwed up his face and took painful hobbling steps across the kitchen. As soon as Aunt Mandy sat down, he helped himself to her cane and began limping around with that.

"That cane belongs to Aunt Mandy," Ray told him.

"And you are not really lame," Benjie said. He was going to stick up for Aunt Mandy's cane. What belonged to Aunt Mandy was Aunt Mandy's!

Danny's face fell. He looked so hurt and sad that Benjie was sorry. Then Benjie thought of something. Without another word he scurried up into the attic.

Soon he returned with a pair of crutches. When he gave these to Danny, Danny's face lit up. A cane was good, but crutches were better. Danny had seen a man on crutches, and he knew how to use them. Now he could let his bad leg be even worse than it had been with the cane.

When Aunt Mandy saw Danny with his crutches, she had to laugh. All the others had to laugh too. Aunt Mandy was so interested in watching Danny hobbling about that she forgot herself and started to stand up. Right away Uncle Albert was at her side and helped her into the living room.

Mom and Aunt Katie were visiting as fast as they could. Dad and Uncle Albert were trying to catch up on all their news. Aunt Mandy was not interested in visiting. She looked about sharply. "Where are we?" she asked.

Benjie was right at her elbow. "You are here," Benjie told her. "Would you go on a walk with us? Please?"

The men stopped talking. "Go on a walk?" Uncle Albert repeated, sounding thoughtful.

He looked at Aunt Katie.

"It might be a good idea," she nodded. Aside, she told Mom, "You'd think she'd be tired, but if she wants to go, it would be good for her."

"We'll help you out," the men offered. Dad and Uncle Albert soon had Aunt Mandy outside. The wheelchair was still sitting in front of the porch.

"Now then," Uncle Albert said cheerfully, "We'll get you settled on here, and the boys can take you around."

Aunt Mandy stiffened. She glared at the wheelchair.

"Who brought that thing?" she demanded. It was plain that she did not like that wheelchair.

Uncle Albert and Dad looked at each other. There was a helpless look on Uncle Albert's face. He knew if he told Aunt Mandy she might fall, she would feel insulted. How could they get Aunt Mandy to like the wheelchair?

Benjie stepped up. "Please, Aunt Mandy. I want to give you a ride," he said. "A real fast ride."

Danny crowded close. Both his legs were 'hurting' now. He was sure he needed the wheelchair.

"Please, Aunt Mandy, let me give you a ride," Benjie persisted.

Aunt Mandy looked at him. She liked to make children happy. "Very well. This boy can give me a fast ride."

Quickly Dad and Uncle Albert settled her on the wheelchair. They did not want to give Aunt Mandy a chance to change her mind.

"I want to give her a ride too," Ray was saying.

"And I want a turn," Ellen chimed in.

"I want a turn," Danny echoed. Suddenly his legs were feeling better.

Aunt Mandy beamed. Being put on a wheelchair because you were old and tottery was very different from being put on it so that children could have the chance of giving you a ride.

"Now then, I am ready," she said. "Now mind you do not fly around the corners."

"Be very careful," Dad said in an undertone to the children. Then they were off. First Benjie had his turn. Aunt Mandy wanted to see everything. Ray walked on one side and Ellen on the other. Danny went back inside to fetch his crutches. It would be more interesting to have a lame leg and use the crutches than to just walk along.

They pushed Aunt Mandy everywhere a wheelchair could go. They told her about the pet ducks Mr. Brown had brought them. Then they had to tell her about the goats eating Aunt Ruth's garden.

Suddenly they noticed that Aunt Mandy had fallen asleep. So now they talked together in whispers, and quietly pushed Aunt Mandy back to the house.

When Aunt Mandy woke up, she was sitting in the wheelchair in front of the porch where the menfolk were chatting. As soon as Dad and Uncle Albert noticed that Aunt Mandy was awake, they helped her into the house. They did not tell her she had had a good nap. Aunt Mandy did not like to take naps.

Aunt Katie was setting the table for supper. Ellen was playing with Ruth and Toby. Mom was just starting to fry eggs for egg sandwiches. Aunt Mandy did not want to sit down. She stood beside Mom.

"How many egg sandwiches do you want?" Mom asked her.

Aunt Mandy's eyebrows went up. "Eggs for supper?"

"Yes. We like them in sandwiches." Mom broke another egg into the skillet. She was frying the eggs in butter, and there was a good smell of butter in the kitchen — butter that was browning lightly.

Aunt Mandy sniffed."But I eat my eggs at breakfast."

"Well, I'm making them for everyone else, and I'd be glad to make you one too." Carefully, Mom turned the eggs in the skillet.

"Not an egg for supper," Aunt Mandy said. But she kept watching Mom fry the eggs.

"So you don't want an egg?" Mom asked, when she flipped the first batch of golden eggs onto a platter.

"Ooh, they smell delicious," Aunt Katie said. They really did. But she was also trying to encourage Aunt Mandy to eat one.

Mom opened another carton of eggs. She knew the children loved egg sandwiches, and so did Uncle Alberts. Silently, Aunt Mandy watched as Mom started frying another skillet of eggs.

"Well, maybe I can eat one after all," Aunt Mandy decided. And instead of just one, Aunt Mandy ate *two* egg sandwiches for supper.

When they were finished eating, Aunt Katie gave Aunt Mandy her pills, putting them beside her plate. Aunt Mandy frowned. "I am not a cow, or a horse," she said. Aunt Mandy felt only a cow or horse could take that many pills.

Ellen counted them. "There are just four," she said.

"Four too many," Aunt Mandy retorted. She did not like to take her pills. "I am going to see the doctor. I will ask him if I have to take all these pills."

Aunt Mandy forgot that she had already been to the doctor. He was the one who had given the pills to Aunt Katie and told her to see to it that Aunt Mandy took them.

Poor Aunt Mandy! She thought it was Aunt Katie's fault that she had to take the pills. She tried to get out of it every way she could.

Later that evening, Aunt Katie told Mom what Aunt Mandy had done the week before. One morning when Aunt Katie went to throw something in the trash, she saw four pills lying in the bottom of the trash can. Surprised, she pulled them out and showed them to Aunt Mandy.

"What pills are these?" Aunt Katie had asked.

"I thought I wouldn't take them this morning," Aunt Mandy had answered.

"So you can see," Aunt Katie told Mom, "why we always watch until she has swallowed her pills. But we dare not leave any pills in her room, either. For if Aunt Mandy can't sleep, she will get up and take any kind of pill she can find."

"She could harm herself if she took an extra blood pressure pill, or any of the others, for that matter," Mom said.

"Yes, she could. So that is why we watch her so closely. But we are glad we are able to take care of Aunt Mandy. It is a privilege to share our home with her."

The next morning Mom made pancakes for breakfast. Everyone remembered that Aunt Mandy liked pancakes. "I am so glad she always has a good appetite," Aunt Katie said. "Usually she enjoys whatever I make."

"She is not the only one with a good appetite," Uncle Albert said, spearing another pancake. Dad passed the sausage again, and Uncle Albert took a second patty. Mom was beaming. She loved to cook and see that everyone had plenty to eat.

Soon after breakfast, Aunt Mandy was on the wheelchair again, and Ray and Benjie took turns pushing her around. Once Benjie almost drove over Engine, the lazy tomcat, who was lying in the sun taking a nap. Of course, Aunt Mandy did not remember Engine, but it did not matter.

"Engine doesn't know the difference," Benjie said.

Chapter 18

Enjoying Company

Ray and Benjie loved to sit and hear Dad and Mom and Uncle Albert and Aunt Katie deep in conversation.

Uncle Albert had planted fruit trees in the spring.

"You would think," Aunt Katie said fondly, "that he would have enough work at his age without planting a lot of extra trees to look after."

Uncle Albert had an interesting little farm. He had a nice pony that a man had once given him. Benjie remembered that pony. It did not have the pep and spunk that Pepper had, but it was a good, safe pony.

Uncle Albert also kept ducks and geese, a few turkeys, some sheep, a cow, and a horse on his farm. He even had a goat or two. He had chickens, bantams, and guineas.

"Yes, but trees are different from animals," Uncle Albert was saying. "They don't get out into your garden or run away. They stay right where you put them."

"That is a good thing," Aunt Katie said, laughing. "We have had so many wild chases on our little farm already."

"But about the trees," she went on, "Albert waters them and puts fertilizer around them and spends a lot of time with those trees."

"Trees are interesting," Uncle Albert agreed, smiling. "And a tree usually lives a long time."

Uncle Albert looked at Ray and Benjie. "Did you know one can compare a tree to a little child. If a young tree is not planted right, or trained right, it will grow up crooked. And once a tree is crooked, you can not straighten it out."

Uncle Albert pulled at his beard thoughtfully. "I'd say trees need good soil, good food, and plenty of water to grow into a healthy tree. Children need a similar environment."

"But trees can't make choices, can they?" Ray said, thinking out loud.

"No indeed," Uncle Albert agreed. "A tree is just that, a tree. But as children grow up, they can make choices. They can choose to be like the tree in Psalm One. There it says a man who thinks about God's Word day and night is 'like a tree, planted by the rivers of water, that bringeth forth his fruit in his season; his leaf also shall not wither, and whatsoever he doeth shall prosper.' "

Uncle Albert paused before going on. "Trees, like people, bring forth fruit," he said. "I know you boys want to be good 'trees' and bring forth good fruit. And that is what I expect from my fruit trees. I may not live to see much fruit on them, but maybe others will. When you plant a tree, you are doing something for the next generations. Think for a minute what it would be like if we had no trees!"

Benjie thought about that. Come to think of it, he loved trees. He enjoyed climbing trees. Birds hid their nests in trees. Squirrels built their homes in trees. Trees gave you shade. They gave you apples and other fruit. You could even use their dead leaves to mulch a garden and enrich the soil.

"Think of all the things trees are used for," Mom was saying. "Paper is made from wood. Furniture, books, pencils . . . it's hard telling what all we get from trees."

"Trees also get chopped down and used for firewood," Dad added. "Wood heats homes and keeps people warm."

"I want to plant a tree!" Benjie said suddenly. "I want to take care of a tree. I want to see how much it grows in a year."

"Yes! Me too!" Ray agreed eagerly. "I would like to plant a nut tree. Maybe a squirrel would move into the tree if it had nuts on it."

"How about eating the nuts yourself?" Aunt Katie asked with a smile.

"The squirrels and I would share."

Ray pondered a little. "But I'd have to decide which kind of nut tree. There are pecan trees, hickory trees, walnut trees . . ." Ray paused to think.

"Chestnut," Uncle Albert added, "and butternut, hazelnut, English walnut, and several other kinds of hickory nuts."

"I never stopped to think how many nut trees there are," Dad said. "And likely there are many more that we haven't mentioned."

"What about coconut trees?" Aunt Katie liked coconut.

"That's right," Uncle Albert agreed, "but we can't raise coconut palm trees here. Have you decided which one you want, Ray?"

"I think I would choose shagbark hickory. Then we would all enjoy the nuts." Ray knew Mom liked hickory nuts for cookies and cakes and pies.

Benjie looked enviously at Ray. It had been easy for Ray to make up his mind. Whether they actually planted trees or not, it was interesting to plan and think about. But what tree would he choose? peach? apple? a shade tree? an evergreen tree? How would he ever make up his mind?

"I think planting trees would be a very good idea," Dad decided. "Ray and Benjie and Ellen can each have time to think what tree they want to plant. I am glad you gave us the idea, Uncle Albert."

Through all this talk, Aunt Mandy had been dozing on the rocking chair. It was easy for Aunt Mandy to nap a little while they talked.

* * * * *

The time passed pleasantly while the Mast family enjoyed their guests' stay. Uncle Albert and Aunt Katie and Aunt Mandy spent a day and a night at Uncle Mark's place too. Then how empty the house seemed! Benjie was not very pleased to share his company with Uncle Marks, though he knew he must not be selfish. How good it felt when the three visitors came back to his house!

Then one evening, Dad and Mom invited Uncle Marks and a few other families over for supper.

Benjie felt both glad and sad. For in a few days, their company, including Danny, would leave for home. Benjie did not know what there was to look forward to when they left. Danny had become a good friend. Aunt Mandy was an old friend. Uncle Albert and Aunt Katie were special old friends too. What would he do when they left? Benjie loved having company.

Danny loved company too. Right away Danny wanted to play church with the visiting children.

So they all gathered together under the big shade tree. It was a warm evening. They could hear the sleepy sound of birds getting ready to roost in the trees for the night. They listened to the sweet piping of crickets. Benjie loved the night sounds.

Ellen brought Danny a glass of water. Danny had to have that! Ray brought a chair to set the glass on. Danny smiled. How he loved an audience! And this evening he was in top form.

He had so much to preach about! He told of the cobbler who fixed his shoe. Then spreading out his hands, he exclaimed, "Benjie let egg plop down on Ellen's head!" Danny covered his face with his hands and pretended to cry, as if he were Ellen. Then he stopped and mightily he cleared his throat. He took a drink. He looked around at his listeners.

"Benjie, stop laughing," he admonished. But that made the children laugh harder than ever.

"Bad goats. Ate strawberries," Danny said, shaking his head. "Children must not let goats out. Bad children to let goats out."

"Ray steal my knife," Danny said sorrowfully. "Ray must not steal. Bible says so."

Danny waved his arms and took another long drink. "Black cow is bad. She kick at Danny."

"Did you let the goats out?" Becky whispered to Alta.

"Oh, no. They broke out when we were not at home."

"Alta, stop whispering." Danny kept a sharp eye on his "church" and he loved to give orders.

"Ray did not steal a knife either," Ellen whispered.

"Bible says sing." Danny raised his arms and started to sing "Jesus Loves Me." He nodded to the children. "Help sing."

So they all pitched in and sang. Then "church" was over. Before anyone realized what Danny was doing, what do you think? He raised his glass, and with a whoosh he splashed the remaining water out over the children. Then what confusion! The children scrambled away, and the grown-ups came to the porch to see what was going on.

Danny was laughing. "Everyone my friend," he said. "Everyone my buddy."

In no time at all it was nearing bedtime. "I wish we could stay all night," Nathan said as he climbed into his father's buggy.

"Now it is your turn to visit us, Ellen," Becky said. "It was a *splendid* evening." Becky loved to use big words.

* * * * *

The next morning Mom could not find her letter from Grandma. "I thought I put it on the shelf," she frowned thoughtfully. "Grandma sent her relish recipe, and I wanted to compare it with yours, Katie."

Aunt Katie looked thoughtful. "I know mine by heart, but don't know hers. Where are the children?"

"They are pushing Aunt Mandy around in the wheelchair, and Danny is hopping about on his crutches."

"I have an idea where your letter is," Aunt Katie said mysteriously. "Let's go look."

Mom looked surprised, but she followed Aunt Katie. They went upstairs to Danny's room.

"Now which is Danny's drawer?" Aunt Katie asked.

"Why, it is this one."

"You open it and look what all he has tucked in there."

Mom pulled open the drawer. Underneath Danny's shirts, she found her missing letter. Mom also found several other letters there that she had forgotten all about. Ellen's pen was hidden there too, and several paper animals that people had given Danny. All the animals had either their heads or tails cut off, for Danny had not liked the way they looked.

Mom rummaged around a little more and found Dad's measuring tape and Benjie's pencil sharpener.

"And we didn't even miss these things!" Mom exclaimed. Then she and Aunt Katie had to laugh. "He reminds me of a pack rat," Mom said. "Whenever he sees something he likes, he forgets that it is wrong to take it."

"And he loves to get mail," Aunt Katie said. "That is why he took your letters."

"We will have to send him a letter when he gets back home," Mom said. "Poor boy. You can't blame him if he wants to get a letter too."

The two women gathered up Danny's stolen treasures and carried them downstairs. When Danny came in to get a drink, limping as if in great pain, Mom showed him the items she had found. "These things do not belong to you, Danny," she said reproachfully.

Danny's face fell. "But I want letter too. I want pen too. Now all mine," he said.

"Don't you remember, Danny? It is wrong to steal," Aunt Katie said.

Danny looked guilty, but hurt. "Poor me. Have no tape. No sharpener. No letter."

Mom put her hand on Danny's shoulder. Her heart went out to him. He looked so crestfallen, so disappointed, and hurt. "Tell you what, Danny," she said. "I will get you a sharpener and a little tape measure all your own. But you must not take things that are not yours."

Danny's face brightened wonderfully. "Mommy friend. My buddy!" he rejoiced. "Aunt Katie my friend. My buddy." He gave them both a hug.

Then he limped happily outside again. "Hundred times sorry," he was saying.

"We are going to miss him so much," Mom

said. She felt like crying. Danny was so innocent, and so much a child. So lovable in spite of his wrongdoings.

"I know," Aunt Katie agreed. "He is so special. Sometimes I imagine how it will be in heaven for Danny. Of course, no one knows exactly, but we can think about it. It seems to me that Danny will burst with happiness and wonder."

"And how he will love everybody!" Mom added, wiping away her tears. "If only we could all be as loving as he is."

"That is right. He never holds grudges. If he feels unhappy, he soon forgets about it," Aunt Katie said. "He does not hide bad feelings in his heart. He shows how he feels and is as open as a book. Dear boy! He has a mission on this earth just like everyone else does."

Chapter 19

Danny's Antics

Uncle Albert loved children, and the children loved him. Whenever he was outside, Ray and Benjie would be right at his heels. He knew so many interesting stories. And he knew such fascinating little tricks. He knew how to make many different kinds of knots in a rope. He knew such a lot of things a boy liked to know!

Danny enjoyed being with Uncle Albert too. But Danny was easily distracted by other things he liked to do. He would soon wander off to check out something else.

Dad had to put a hook on the henhouse door out of Danny's reach. For Danny loved to go into the henhouse. Even though Dad told him not to, Danny would forget.

"Found two eggs," he would say. As soon as a few eggs were laid, Danny wanted to get them.

And since he was clumsy, he often dropped one or two. Of course when Ray or Benjie fed the hens, Danny could go into the henhouse with them. If two hens were on one nest, Danny would scold those hens.

Danny loved to imagine things. Every week, the Mast family got a newspaper called *The Budget* delivered to their house. On Saturday, when *The Budget* came, Danny loved to sit down and pretend he was reading the news. On this Saturday morning, Danny had *The Budget*. The children (and even the grown-ups) enjoyed listening to Danny's imaginary news.

Danny sat bolt upright in the rocking chair, holding up *The Budget*. He squinted intently at the front page.

"Oh, is awful!" he exclaimed.

"What happened?" Ray asked eagerly.

"Big baby. Ten pounds!"

"Whose baby is it?"

Danny looked at *The Budget* closely. "Adam Mast's."

"What is the baby's name?" Benjie asked.

"His name is Benjie!" Danny exclaimed, and then he laughed. He loved to tease Benjie.

"What else does *The Budget* say?" Ellen asked, coming closer to Danny.

"Bishop was in church."

"What is his name?"

"No name." Danny shook his head and peered at his paper again.

"Oh! Poor man!" he exclaimed next.

"What happened now?" one of the grown-ups asked. The adults had been visiting, but they found Danny's "news" too interesting to ignore.

"Jake's Joe fall in river." Danny clucked his tongue in sympathy.

"Well, I wonder how that happened," Dad said, playing along.

Danny squinted at *The Budget* again. "Jake push him."

"That would be wrong to push someone!" Aunt Katie exclaimed.

"Indeed, yes," everyone agreed.

"Hundred times sorry," Danny said, pretending to read again.

"Oh, is bad!" Danny exclaimed next.

"Now what?" Benjie peered over Danny's shoulder.

"Man steal knife."

"That *is* bad," Uncle Albert said. "The Bible says we must not steal."

Soon Danny laid *The Budget* down. Now he was ready for the *Freundschaft Buch*. This was a book that had all the descendants of the Mast family recorded in it. Danny would pore over these pages and rattle off funny-sounding names that no one had ever heard before.

Danny spoke mostly Pennsylvania Dutch. He

176

could speak only a few words in English. But he thought he could speak English as well as anyone else.

That afternoon Dad went to the other end of the community to buy some things at a store. Uncle Albert and the boys went along.

On the way, they stopped at Emory Byler's place to return a tool Dad had borrowed. To their surprise, they saw Al Camp there, cleaning out a fence row.

When Al looked up and saw them, a big smile spread over his face.

"Why, I think he is really glad to see us!" Benjie exclaimed. "Maybe we are his friends after all."

"We are glad to see you again," Dad told Al.

Eagerly Danny pushed close to Al. "What doing?" he asked.

Al looked at Danny. He had never met Danny before.

What will Al think of Danny? Benjie wondered silently. *Maybe Al will think Danny is rude.*

But there was no need to worry. Never had they seen such a big smile on Al Camp's face as they saw now, when he looked at Danny. It was plain to see that Al liked Danny right away, even if he had never seen him before.

"Why, I am cleaning out this fence row," Al explained kindly, in English. "And what is your name?"

Danny beamed. It made him feel very important when someone talked to him in English.

"My name is Danny," he answered.

Ray and Benjie were listening a little anxiously. They were afraid Al would not understand Danny's mixed-up Dutch and English words. But Al nodded to show he understood.

Danny was not finished. "What your name?" he asked.

Al's smile widened. "My name is Al. Al Camp."

He pulled out his big red handkerchief and wiped his face.

"Where do you live?" he asked. This time Danny did not understand what Al asked. But it did not matter.

"You my friend. My buddy," he announced. "Al smart man. Work hard," he added, in a funny mixture of English and Dutch. Al smiled and smiled.

"Are you staying a while longer in the community?" Dad asked Al as they started to leave.

"Maybe a while," Al answered, "if I have work." Al looked at Uncle Albert. In his slow way he asked, "You don't live here, do you?"

"No, I don't," Uncle Albert replied, surprised. How had Al known that he did not live in this community?

"Has Al met all the people here, or how did he

178

know I don't live here?" Uncle Albert asked after they were on their way again.

Dad shook his head. "Al is sharp. He notices little things. But I don't know how he knew. I can't imagine he has met everyone living here."

"Well, that is interesting. And he stays as long as he has work?"

"Maybe he should have said he stays as long as he has cake and pie," Ray said, laughing.

"And bread. Homemade bread," Benjie added.

"Smart man," Danny was saying. "Al work hard."

When they got back home later in the afternoon, Danny pretended to be Al. He found one of Dad's big handkerchiefs in the drawer. No one told him where they were kept, but Danny knew. Danny was sharp too. He wiped his face like Al had done. Then he pretended he was working like Al. He hobbled around the kitchen table and pretended to hack down weeds.

"Al walk like this," he said.

"I thought you were lame and had to use crutches," Benjie teased.

You never knew what answer Danny would come up with. He looked at Benjie and frowned.

"Benjie, stop talking bad," he scolded.

"I wasn't talking bad," Benjie protested. But he knew he had teased Danny just to see what he would say.

"Benjie not my friend. Not my buddy." Danny pouted. "Just Ray and Ellen my friend." Danny was not in the mood to be reminded about being lame. Right now he wanted to be Al Camp and no one else. As far as Danny was concerned, he had never used crutches!

"Now, Benjie, stop bothering Danny," Mom reproved.

"Danny, you know you like Benjie," Aunt Katie spoke up.

Suddenly Benjie had an idea. "Danny is *my* friend," he announced. "Danny is my buddy."

Danny smiled, his troubles forgotten. "Benjie work hard. Benjie my friend."

Danny spread out his arms. "Everyone my friend!"

Then a mischievous look came into Danny's eye. "All but Aunt Katie," he said.

"But you like Aunt Katie too," Mom reminded Danny. She knew he just wanted to see what she would say.

But Danny pretended he did not want Aunt Katie for his friend. Aunt Katie was not hurt. She knew Danny liked the attention he was getting.

* * * * *

"Mom," Benjie whispered, looking around to be sure no one else was nearby.

"Benjie, I thought you were in bed." Mom looked concerned. "Are you sick?"

180

"Oh, no," Benjie shook his head, "I am not sick. But I can't sleep."

"Can't sleep? Did you do something you shouldn't have?"

"No, Mom." Benjie sniffed a little. "But what am I going to do when Danny goes home? And Aunt Mandy and Uncle Alberts too? But Danny was here the longest so I will miss him the mostest."

"You mean you will miss him the most," Mom corrected. "But yes, I know. We are all going to miss Danny."

Mom paused to look at her troubled son. "Benjie, do you remember how you felt when Danny opened your box trap?"

Of course Benjie remembered. He remembered he could hardly wait to catch a rabbit. He and Danny checked the trap morning and evening, but there was no rabbit. Finally, when he had given up hope of ever catching one, Danny came in one morning all excited.

"Rabbit! Rabbit!" he kept exclaiming.

Ray and Benjie hurried out to the orchard. For once that morning, Benjie had waited until after breakfast to check his trap, but Danny did not wait. When the boys got to the trap, the trapdoor was open.

"Rabbit jump out!" Danny said. "Rabbit go hop, hop fast, like this." And Danny hopped as fast as he could through the orchard grass.

For once Benjie felt very cross with Danny. Now, when he finally had caught a rabbit, Danny had let it go!

"But what would you have done with the rabbit?" Dad asked Benjie later. "Would you have wanted to kill it and eat it?" Dad knew what Benjie would say.

"Kill my rabbit?!" Benjie exclaimed, horrified. "I would never kill it!"

"Well, it is much happier being out of the trap and hopping about than it would be if you had it penned up."

Benjie knew that Dad was right, but still he wished to hold his rabbit, one wild rabbit, for a little while.

"If you could catch some very small rabbits, that would be better," Dad advised. "Even so, it is hard to raise wild bunnies. But maybe next time." Dad felt sorry for Benjie.

"And you must not blame Danny," he continued. "It was very special to him to find that rabbit. He has been preaching about it ever since." Dad smiled. "Likely you'll catch another one with those big carrots you dig up."

Yes, Benjie did remember how he had felt when Danny opened his trap. But now he knew he would not mind if Danny opened it and let another rabbit hop away. A rabbit was *just* a rabbit, but Danny was Danny. And Monday morning they were planning to leave—Uncle

Alberts, Aunt Mandy, and Danny.

"I'm glad you love Danny," Mom said, "and because you love him, you can forget the wrong things he did. Forgive and forget. But before Danny came, you didn't know you would have such a friend. And who knows? There are a lot of new friends you haven't met yet. And you will want to try to be better friends with the friends you do have. Since Danny has been here, you aren't with Enos much on Sunday, or the other boys. You want to cultivate your friendship with them too."

"Cultivate friendship," Benjie repeated. He liked that. He knew what cultivate meant. You cultivated the field to plant corn. You cultivated to get the weeds out. You cultivated to get some seeds down deep so they would grow deep roots.

"Now you need to get to bed, Benjie," Mom said. "And if you don't understand about cultivating friendships, Dad can explain it better tomorrow. You think about it, and remember to be just as friendly and kind as you can be to everyone you meet."

"Because maybe they are all waiting to be my friends?"

"Yes, old and young, no matter what their age. Everyone needs friends. And being friendly and kind is about the best way to cultivate friendships."

"And it doesn't cost anything to be kind, does it?" Benjie knew it was bedtime, but as long as he could get Mom to talk, he stalled off going. Besides, he really was interested in cultivating friendships.

"It doesn't cost anything to say a kind word or share a smile," Mom said. "Now run along to bed, Benjie. Good night!"

"Yes, Mom. Good night, Mom. Sleep tight."

Chapter 20

Benjie's "No Work" Plan

"**I** wish Danny had never come."

"Why, Benjie!" Mom exclaimed, shocked. "I thought you loved Danny!" Mom looked closely at her son. She could not remember when Benjie had ever had such a long face. Truly, he looked like he had lost his best friend. What had come over him?

"If Danny had never come, then I wouldn't miss him now," Benjie said mournfully.

It was Monday morning. The visitors had left right after an early breakfast. Now, the whole house seemed to have a lonely, empty feeling since they were gone. Benjie hardly knew what to do with himself.

"It won't seem right ever again," he said.

"Everywhere I go I miss Danny."

"And you miss Aunt Mandy?" Mom asked.

"Oh, yes, I miss Aunt Mandy, too. And Uncle Alberts."

"Maybe we can find someone to take Aunt Mandy's place. Enos's grandfather Mose is here this summer, remember? Have you tried to be friends with him? That is a friendship to cultivate."

Benjie shook his head. He did not want to think about cultivating friendships with anyone but his own friends. "I just want Danny and Aunt Mandy and Uncle Alberts," he repeated.

Mom ignored Benjie's dark mood. "I imagine old Mose knows some interesting stories. I want to have him and Enos's family over for a meal sometime soon. It will be enjoyable to hear what he has to say."

Mom smiled at Benjie. They *all* missed Aunt Mandy and Uncle Alberts and Danny. Ray and Ellen were accepting the change. They had known Danny would leave, and that was that. But Benjie was different.

Benjie felt cheerless and unhappy and lonesome. He did not smile back at Mom. The house was too quiet. The barn was too quiet. He did not want to be anywhere! Poor Benjie. Even knowing that the old mother cat, Caboose, had a nest of kittens in the hayloft did not interest him.

After dinner, Dad read a story to the children

as a special treat. The story was about a boy named Sammy who did not want to work. Benjie listened with only part of his mind. How could he enjoy a story when all his friends had left?

Everyone, even Ray and Ellen, had tried to cheer Benjie, but Benjie did not want to be cheered. He did not feel like working. He did not feel like playing. He did not feel like doing anything except brooding over his troubles.

But what was Dad reading? Sammy did not want to work. By the time Dad was finished reading the story, Benjie decided he did not want to work either, and he said so.

"What do you mean, you do not want to work anymore?" Dad asked. Usually Benjie was the one who was eager to get a job done. "Well, Mom and I will talk about this and let you know what we decide."

"Mom," Dad said later, when they were alone, "I don't think it is a good idea. Benjie needs something to do, to keep him from moping around."

Mom looked thoughtful. "Ever since Danny came, Benjie had been going in high gear. Now his time feels so empty. He does need something."

Mom paused to think. "Something to occupy him," she mused. "But maybe . . ." Mom had an idea. She shared it with Dad, and they agreed to try it.

187

So that evening Dad announced that Benjie could have a week without work.

* * * * *

The next morning, Benjie started to get up with Ray to help chore.

"Oh, no, Benjie. You stay in bed. No chores for you. Remember?" Ray said quickly.

So Benjie lay back in bed. But he had not realized how strange he would feel lying in bed while Ray went with Dad to do the chores.

"How do you like it?" Ellen asked Benjie at breakfast.

"Of course I like it!" Benjie said.

After breakfast he played with little Toby in the sandbox. Now he could play all he wanted to, and no one would interrupt to ask for his help! He wondered what Danny would say if he could see him. Danny would call him a lazy boy. Benjie was sure of it.

Dad and Ray were loading up supplies to fix the back fence. Then they wanted to put some rocks in the lane that went through the woods. When it rained, the lane got terribly muddy. That did not do when you wanted to drive through the woods!

"Could I go along to watch?" Benjie asked hopefully.

"I'm sorry, Benjie," Dad replied,"but the understanding was that you stay around the house. If you went along with us, you would likely forget yourself and start working."

Already Benjie was wishing he had never thought of his "no work" plan. Benjie stayed at the sandbox, but he did not enjoy playing like he had expected to. He kept wondering what Dad and Ray were doing. He wondered so much that he forgot to think about how much he missed Danny and the others.

What a long forenoon that was! Finally dinner was ready, and Dad and Ray came back from the woods.

"Did you finish the job?" Mom asked them at the table.

Benjie listened anxiously. He hoped it would take weeks to get the lane fixed. Surely he could still go next week . . .

"Oh, no, we are not finished yet," Dad said cheerfully. "And we miss Benjie's help."

"Will it take another week?" Benjie asked hopefully.

"It depends how much time we get to work on it."

"Danny would have enjoyed going along," Benjie said in a small voice.

"Yes, he would have," Dad agreed.

After dinner Benjie lay on the grass under the shade tree. He did not have to help with the dishes. He would not have to help do the chores. Soon Benjie was fast asleep.

"He is tired out," Mom said. "We do not want to waken him." And Benjie did not wake up until Ray and Dad started doing chores late that afternoon.

The next day seemed even longer than the first day had been. Benjie played with Toby and Baby Ruth, but he was tired of playing. He was tired of himself.

"Why don't you read a book?" Mom suggested. "Or color a picture?"

But Benjie did not want to read a book. He did not want to color a picture. Not in the summertime when he could be outside! Besides, Benjie was feeling a little cross with the Sammy story. After all, that was what had given him the idea of not working.

"Uncle Mark's cherry tree has a lot of ripe cherries," Mom said the next morning. "They said we can come and pick all we want."

Dad and Ray had just come in for breakfast. Benjie was already seated at the table. Quickly he sat up straight. Picking cherries at Uncle Marks?

"I thought it might suit to go over today," Mom continued. "Ruth says the birds are after those cherries too. They'll get them if we don't."

"Well," Dad said, "if it suits you and the children to go, that's fine with me. I'll need to stay home and go on with my work."

Benjie swallowed hard. They would go pick

cherries and have a wonderful time, and he would be at home, doing nothing!

"I—I want to go too!" Benjie burst out. "I am tired of not working! Please let me go and help." He winked back tears. "I can't stand another lazy day."

Dad thought a bit. "You are sure you want to help with the chores again? You really want to work? Your week isn't up yet, but it is your choice. If you go along to pick cherries, it means you go back to work."

"Yes!" Benjie said, relieved. "Please let me go."

"Of course you may," Mom said. She reached over to squeeze his shoulder. "We are glad you want to work again."

"I missed your help," Dad added. "We needed another little man down in the woods with those stones."

"And I, for one, am glad too!" Ray said. "It's not fun getting up by myself to chore."

After breakfast, everyone flew around.The dishes were washed in record time. When that was done, Benjie swept the kitchen. He had a good feeling inside. A feeling of worth, of usefulness. It felt so good to work, and he had never realized it before. Carefully, he carried out the scraps for the cats. They were not very hungry, for they were always given some milk when the men milked the cows.

191

Skipper, however, was always hungry. Growing pups can eat and eat. Sometimes Shep would sniff at a pile of scraps or bones and not bother to eat them. But if Skipper came, Shep would start to chew on them. And if Skipper came too close, Shep would growl a warning. *These are my bones,* the growl would say. Even though he and Skipper were friends now, it did not work to have the two dogs eat together. The boys always made two separate piles of bones: one pile for Shep and one pile for Skipper.

Now Skipper came running and gulped down the scraps the cats didn't want. Skipper did not even bother to chew his food.

Sometimes Mom wished they had never kept Skipper. He made holes in the flower beds. Several times he had chased the hens and once he had caught one. Likely he would have killed it if Ray had not been right there. Then Skipper was spanked and tied up for a day. But he was learning. He no longer chased the chickens, though you could see he wanted to.

He loved to go with Benjie to fetch the cows. Even in the early, dewy morning, he was eager to go. Usually Shep went along too. Together the dogs would scare up a rabbit or two, but they never could catch any. And Benjie was glad.

As soon as the morning work was done, Mom and the children went to Uncle Mark's place. Uncle Marks had already picked many cherries, but there were still many more on the tree. Even though Aunt Ruth had sewing to do, she came out and helped them.

"It is so enjoyable to do something together like this," Aunt Ruth said. Of course, Nathan and Alta were eager to help too.

Right away Aunt Ruth asked if they had heard the news.

"What news?" they chorused. They all looked expectantly at Aunt Ruth.

Her eyes twinkled at Ray and Benjie. "Harvey and Enos have a baby brother. He was born last evening," she announced. She started picking cherries again. "Don't you think this will make them happy?"

Benjie thought about Enos. *Yes, Enos would be happy with a baby brother.*

"Remember how Harvey and Enos scared Pepper?" Ray was asking. "Harvey likes to ask me if Pepper has had any scares lately."

"I hope they know better than to do something like that again," Mom said.

Aunt Ruth nodded. "I should say! Someone could have been hurt, or Pepper could have had a heart attack."

Ray and Benjie looked at each other and grinned. Of course they knew better than to do such a trick. But it *had* been exciting.

"I wonder what the baby's name is," Ellen said. She loved babies.

"They named him Andrew Moses, after his two grandfathers. That will please old Mose," Aunt Ruth answered. She had been happy to find out about this new baby. "Harvey was here this morning to borrow the rake and he told us. He had the biggest smile I've ever seen on Harvey."

"I wish we could tell Danny!" Benjie said. "He would want to know how big the baby is and how he looks."

"You boys will have to write him a letter," Aunt Ruth suggested.

"Danny loves to get mail," Mom reminded them. "And Uncle Alberts can read the letters to him and Aunt Mandy."

Benjie did not like to write letters, but he did not complain. Somehow even writing letters seemed better than doing nothing at all.

I do not want another empty day in my life, he thought to himself. He thought of sick children who could not work and play, and he knew he was very fortunate that he could. *How did they ever get through their day?*

Benjie felt so thankful that he was healthy and strong. He wanted to show Dad and Mom how hard he could work. When Nathan and Ray took time off from cherry picking to go check Nathan's box trap, Benjie did not go along, even though they invited him to.

Then Ellen and Alta went to see if Neil was

awake, and they stopped to look at Alta's new book. Mom and Aunt Ruth went inside to taste some fruit bars Aunt Ruth had made. Of course, Aunt Ruth brought a taste out for everyone.

"These are so good!" Mom said. "And they look unusual. Where did you get your recipe?"

Aunt Ruth gave Mom a quizzical look. Then she laughed. "It's the recipe I got from you," she answered. "No wonder they are good."

They all laughed while Mom shook her head. "But I think they are better than mine," she marveled. She took another bite.

"We like the raspberry filling," Aunt Ruth said, "but, of course, any fruit filling is good."

Benjie stopped very briefly to eat and have a drink. Then he went right back to work. Nimbly, he climbed the branches of the tree and picked cherries as fast as he could. Every now and then he popped a sour cherry into his mouth. He didn't really like sour cherries, but he still wanted to eat one every now and then. Mom would make pies and cobblers with them. As Benjie picked, he could almost taste how good the red cherries would be.

When they were finished picking cherries, they discovered that Benjie had picked the most! Benjie smiled and smiled. He was glad none of his family had mentioned that he had not wanted to work that week. Sometime he would tell Nathan about it. But for now, he did not want to think about how unhappy he had felt.

"All those cherries!" Dad exclaimed, when he saw how many they brought home. "Did you pay for them?"

"Pay for them?!" Mom exclaimed. "You know Uncle Marks better than that! They would not let us pay for these cherries. But I hope when our Red Delicious apple tree is ready to pick, we can share with them. And Aunt Ruth loves our Smokehouse apples for canning."

"Well, we certainly want to share with them in return," Dad agreed.

"Benjie picked the most cherries," Ellen said.

Dad looked at Benjie and smiled. Benjie felt happy all over.

Chapter 21

Special Friends
at Home

"**B**enjie, I'm glad you are not a sloth today," Ray said the next morning.

"Sloth?" Benjie sounded puzzled.

"It means someone who is idle or lazy, or doesn't want to work," Ray explained. "We compare the person to a sloth. Haven't you heard the expression, 'don't be slothful'?"

"I suppose I have."

"But a sloth is actually a kind of animal," Ray said.

"Have you ever seen one?" Benjie asked curiously. "And why didn't you tell me?"

"No, I never have. Sloths live in Central and South America." Ray had been poring over the encyclopedia. "They are very hard to raise in our country. I doubt that there are any even in the zoos."

"Well, why are lazy people compared to sloths?"

"Because sloths move so slowly. How long do you think it takes them to eat one leaf?"

"Hmmmmm. Maybe five minutes?" Benjie guessed.

"No." Ray said the word in English *and* in sign language and shook his head, grinning. "It takes them thirty minutes!"

Benjie looked surprised. "Thirty minutes!" He gave a low whistle. "Whew! Well, how big is the leaf? The size of an elephant?"

"It doesn't say. Well, it says it's a cepropia leaf. It compares in size to a palmetto leaf, like the horse chestnut. Now I'd like to look up those trees and see how their leaves look." Ray took the encyclopedia over to show Benjie the picture. "See the sloth? It can walk upside down hanging from branches, and it can even sleep upside down like that."

Benjie peered at the picture. "It looks strange."

"Yes. They have almost no tail or ears. They hardly ever come down to the ground. They live in trees and eat leaves and twigs and stuff like that."

"Well, it's no wonder!" Benjie exclaimed. "If it takes them half an hour to eat one leaf, it proba-bly takes up all their time just to eat. So they might as well stay in the tree."

"They have time to sleep," Ray reminded him. He took the book back and put it in the bookcase. "So now you know. Sloths move so slowly that if a person is slow or lazy it reminds one of a sloth. So we don't want to be slothful," Ray concluded, sounding industrious.

And Benjie agreed. When he had gotten up that morning, his first thought was that Danny was not there. Then next he thought that he wanted to work with all his might.

Dad and Mom had taught their children that the first thing to do when you wake up is to thank God. There are so many things to thank Him for. The good night's rest. His love and protection through the night. And most of all, His Son Jesus. And today Benjie was very thankful. Even if the house did seem quiet and empty.

Just then Dad came into the room. "Boys, have you decided what kind of tree you want to plant?" he asked.

Ray and Benjie looked at each other. *So Dad had been serious about the trees!*

"You may look through this catalog," Dad said. "Then we will send for whatever kind you want. Each of you and Ellen may choose one."

Benjie and Ray paged through the catalog.

"I want an apple tree," Benjie suddenly decided. He knew they had apple trees in the orchard, but having his own tree would be special. Benjie loved apples, and apple trees were easy to climb.

"Apple trees seem like my friends," Benjie said. "I want a good, friendly apple tree." Already he imagined himself picking apples from his very own tree.

"And I want a hickory tree," Ray stated. "Then Mom can make nut pies and nut cakes and cookies."

"And apple pies with my apples," Benjie added.

When Mom heard the boys' choices, she was very pleased. She loved to bake for her family. Now she was trying to help Ellen decide what tree *she* wanted. Finally Ellen decided on a shade tree.

"We have a good selection," Dad said approvingly. "Maybe Mom and I will pick out a few as well, and we can plant them all along the lane." Dad rose and picked up his hat. "I have a few calls to make; then when I come back we should work on the lane in the woods again."

Benjie smiled. It was what he hoped Dad would plan to do today. Working in the woods made the day go faster.

But Dad was not finished telling his plans. "I think I'll take Benjie with me. He can hold the horse while I go into the store. And Ray, I'll let you help Mom till we get back."

Benjie looked anxiously at Ray. He was

delighted that *he* was the one to go with Dad. But Ray did not look disappointed. Ray was reading another book in his spare time. Perhaps, if he worked fast, he would have time to read in it before Dad and Benjie came home. So Ray was quite cheerful when Dad and Benjie left.

As they drove off in the wagon, Dad talked about his plans for how to fix the lane. Benjie nodded. He loved when Dad talked to him, man to man. It was the way Dad was. He liked to tell Ray and Benjie his plans for the day, and ask them if they had any ideas. It gave Benjie a warm, happy, worthwhile feeling—the feeling that even if he did not have a good idea about something, it still mattered to Dad to know how he felt.

At the grocery store, Dad tied the horse so Benjie could go inside too. A lady with a dog on a leash was approaching them on the sidewalk. Benjie stopped to look at the dog, while Dad went into the store.

"He doesn't bite," the lady said reassuringly.

The dog was jumping and tugging at his leash. He wanted to run about. Benjie thought the dog looked like Skipper. Maybe it was Skipper's brother or sister, but there was no way to find out. It would be rude to ask the lady if her husband had dumped a puppy.

Benjie looked up in time to see Elizabeth, the deaf girl from school, and her mother coming out of the store. Elizabeth's mother knew the lady with the dog, and began chatting with her. Benjie had never talked to Elizabeth before. Now, suddenly, Benjie was glad he knew some sign language. Elizabeth looked so kind and friendly and happy. Her brown eyes sparkled.

She looked at the dog and then at Benjie. Then she signed to him, "I like dogs."

And Benjie signed back, "The dog does not . . ." then Benjie stopped. What was the sign for bite? Quickly he finger-spelled the letters in sign language, b-i-t-e.

Elizabeth laughed. Then she signed, "We have a little dog at home."

Benjie nodded. Then he signed, "We have two dogs." He wanted to tell her that Skipper looked like this dog. But he did not know how to sign all the words, and finger-spelling would take too long.

Elizabeth's mother was saying good-bye to the other lady. Then she turned and smiled at Benjie. "It makes Elizabeth happy when she can talk to her friends," her mother said softly before they walked on.

Slowly, Benjie went into the store. *Why, he was one of Elizabeth's friends!* It was a new thought. *It did not matter that she was older than he was. And he had been able to talk in sign language.* It gave him a good feeling.

Dad was checking out. He smiled when he

saw Benjie. Benjie picked up a sack of groceries to carry out.

"Was there anything you needed?" Dad asked in a low voice as they started out. "If there is, we can still get it."

Benjie could not think of anything. "Mom wanted toothpaste," he remembered.

"Yes, I got that," Dad replied. "So we're all set."

They put the groceries in the back, and Benjie held the lines while Dad untied the horse. Then he let Benjie drive until they came to the next place where Dad wanted to stop.

When they got home, Mom was glad to hear that Benjie was able to talk to Elizabeth. They all had to laugh when they remembered how Danny had talked in sign language. He made all kinds of signs and motions with his hands, but no one could really understand his version of sign language!

Then Mom told them about Harvey and Enos's baby brother. Little Andrew Moses was a Down syndrome baby.

"You mean like Danny?" Ray asked.

Mom nodded. "Maybe in a week or so we can go visit them."

"He must be a very special baby," Benjie said.

"He is," Dad agreed. "But every baby is special. Very special. This baby is uniquely special, for he will always be innocent."

203

"Did they want this kind of baby?" Ellen asked.

"No, it is normal and natural that parents hope their children will be healthy in mind and body. But God knows what is best. He has a purpose and a plan. God makes no mistakes. Down syndrome children can bring a lot of happiness in their own way. Usually they are not as healthy and need more care."

"Yes," Mom said. "And little Andrew Moses is not a big baby. He weighed only six pounds."

"Danny would say, 'Is awful, so tiny,' " Benjie said, taking a deep breath. He could hardly wait to see this baby! This very special baby. He wished — oh, how he wished — that Danny could see the baby too. *Would Danny realize the baby was like him?*

"If Danny finds out, he will pretend he read about it in *The Budget,*" Ellen said.

"It is true that these children often bring more cares to the parents, healthwise," Mom explained, "but they do not bring heartaches."

"How do you mean?" Benjie asked.

"Sometimes 'normal' children grow up and are not obedient. They may reject their parents, and even the Lord, and lead sinful lives."

"Danny would never do something like that!" Benjie said.

"No," Dad agreed, shaking his head. "These children will never do that. Children who leave home to take their own way cause untold heartache and grief. That is much, much worse for parents than having a child who is not healthy in his mind or body."

"I see," Ray said. "That's why we say their innocence is special."

* * * * *

Two weeks later, on a Sunday evening, the Mast family went to see the new baby.

"We don't want to stay long," Mom said in an undertone as they got off the buggy. "We don't want to tire the family, for likely they have been getting a lot of company."

"Come right on in," Enos's father, Reuben, invited from the open doorway.

In the bedroom, Enos's mother, Rachel, was holding the baby and rocking him gently. Right away Toby wanted to hold the baby. And Baby Ruth tried to reach for him too.

Benjie looked and looked at the tiny baby. He did not notice that the baby's mother had an anxious, worried look on her face.

"Please," said Benjie, "I want to see his little hand."

Carefully, the mother opened the tiny hand.

"It is a special little hand!" Benjie exclaimed. "Just like Danny's! God did not forget."

Benjie stared at the baby in wonder. He quite forgot that anyone else was around. "Now I will have another special little friend," he said softly.

"You will indeed," the mother smiled. There was a new light in her eyes.

"And he will never run away and give you heartaches," Ellen said.

Mom looked slightly uneasy. She did not want the children to say something that might worry the baby's mother.

"That is true," Enos's mother said, smiling. She looked at Benjie. "And what did God not forget?"

"Why, the baby's hand. The line that goes across here." Benjie showed her on his own hand. "See? Ours are crooked, but his is straight. And Danny's is straight."

"Maybe it is because these children stay on the straight and narrow way," Ray observed, looking sober.

"That is a new thought," Mother Rachel said. She looked at Mom, who was holding the baby. "I am so glad you came." She stopped and wiped a few tears away.

Enos was pulling Benjie's sleeve. "Come play for a while before you have to leave," he invited.

"Where is Harvey?" Ray asked, as he and Benjie went out with Enos.

"He went for a walk. But he would have stayed if he had known you were coming." Harvey was older than Ray, but he enjoyed being with the younger boys.

In the bedroom, Rachel and Mom continued talking. "It was something to adjust to—having a baby that is not normal," Rachel said.

"Yes," Mom agreed. "I think every mother hopes for a healthy baby."

"Yes," Rachel replied. "But we love him. We know there is a reason for his life. But I have the feeling that some people pity us. And we do not want pity. We are thankful God saw fit to trust us with this baby. But when visitors come and look sad, it wears one down. It makes me happy to know how your children feel about him," Rachel said. "Don't get me wrong. Most people try to be understanding, but to think, Benjie is already looking forward to having him for a friend!"

In the living room, the men were having a good little visit too. But soon it was time to go home.

On the way home, Benjie tried to count up his friends. "I can hardly keep track of them all!" he said.

"Well," Ray helped him out, "there is Aunt Mandy."

"Yes. She is very special."

"Then there is Tobias, our other tramp."

"He is a special friend too," Benjie agreed.

"And there is Al Camp, and the cobbler . . ."

"And they are unusually special friends!"

"Then there is Danny, and Enos, and this baby, and Uncle Alberts . . ."

Benjie rubbed his head. "They are extra special, too."

Dad turned around from the buggy seat up front.

"Benjie, you'll just have to think that every friend you have is *special*. Every friend is different, and special in his own way. That makes life interesting."

Benjie smiled into the darkness. He felt warm and happy and content, there in the back seat of the buggy. Ray was on one side of him and Ellen on the other.

He thought about little Andrew Moses. It would be interesting to see how he grew. Benjie could hold him and play with him and think of Danny.

"You forgot about Elizabeth," Ellen was saying. "She is a friend."

"I can be friendly to Elizabeth with sign language. And I will try to be the best friend I can to everybody," Benjie said.

"Yes," Dad agreed from the front seat. Then he quoted, "A man that has friends must show himself friendly."

"Have compassion for the stranger you meet, just like the Good Samaritan did," Mom added. She turned around to smile at the children. "That will make it easier for you to understand and love them."

"Through Jesus' great love for us, we want to

reach out and love others," Dad said. "That is our aim in life, that others can learn to love Jesus through us."

"I hope I can always have compassion," Ray said thoughtfully. He liked that word, compassion. It was not always easy to love a person immediately, but you could start with compassion, and love would come.

Benjie looked at Ray admiringly. He could always depend on Ray to do the right thing. No matter what happened, Ray would be his strong older brother. Benjie thought of the box trap Ray had made for him.What would he do without Ray?

Suddenly Benjie felt like shouting. "Ray is the best friend I have!" he burst out.

"Of course, Ellen is a best friend too," he added quickly. What would he do without his sister Ellen?

He looked at Dad, who was carefully driving the horse. He looked at Mom, who was holding Ruth, with Toby nestled beside her.

Dad had said a man who has friends must show himself friendly. Who was more friendly than Dad and Mom? Who but Dad and Mom comforted and helped him? They always had time to listen. Why, he would rather talk to Dad and Mom than anyone else. Didn't that make them the best friends of all?

"My very best friends are Dad and Mom!"

Benjie exclaimed. "Everyone on this buggy is my best friend!"

Dad turned to smile at Benjie. "That makes us all happy, Benjie. And the *very best* friend for all of us is . . ." Dad paused to let the children answer.

"It is Jesus!" Ray and Benjie and Ellen said, together.

Benjie was thinking out loud. "My home is where my best friends are. And Jesus is the best friend of all."

"And our real home is in heaven," added Ray. "And that is the best."

"The very best," said Benjie, nodding. "And the most special, because there we can be with *all* our best friends, including the very Best One of all."

Christian Light Publications, Inc., is a nonprofit, conservative Mennonite publishing company providing Christ-centered, Biblical literature including books, Gospel tracts, Sunday school materials, summer Bible school materials, and a full curriculum for Christian day schools and homeschools. Though produced primarily in English, some books, tracts, and school materials are also available in Spanish.

For more information about the ministry of CLP or its publications, or for spiritual help, please contact us at:

Christian Light Publications, Inc.
P. O. Box 1212
Harrisonburg, VA 22803-1212

Telephone—540-434-0768
Fax—540-433-8896
E-mail—info@clp.org
www.clp.org